ALL MY SINS REMEMBERED

ALL MY SINS REMEMBERED

ROD MILLER

FIVE STAR
A part of Gale, a Cengage Company

GALE
A Cengage Company

LIBRARY OF CONGRESS CATALOGING-IN-PUBLICATION DATA

Names: Miller, Rod, 1952- author.
Title: All my sins remembered / Rod Miller.
Description: First edition. | [Waterville] : Five Star, 2022. | Sum-
    mary: Identifiers: LCCN 2021035970 | ISBN 9781432887285
    (hardcover)
Subjects: LCGFT: Novels.
Classification: LCC PS3613.I55264 A78 2022 | DDC 813/.54—
    dc23
LC record available at https://lccn.loc.gov/2021035970

First Edition. First Printing: February 2022
Find us on Facebook—https://www.facebook.com/FiveStarCengage
Visit our website—http://www.gale.cengage.com/fivestar
Contact Five Star Publishing at FiveStar@cengage.com

Printed in Mexico
Print Number: 01   Print Year: 2022

ALL MY SINS REMEMBERED

—William Shakespeare, *Hamlet*

CHAPTER ONE

He reined up his horse atop the saddleback pass and sat watching, shimmering through the heat waves like a mirage. He came on down the road. The horse's hoof falls kept time with the squeak of the windmill. I did not recognize the man nor his mount. With no hint from the rider, the horse stopped near enough for palaver but not so close as to bode any ill. The rider stacked his hands on the horn of the saddle and watched me. I watched him.

"You are a long ways from somewhere, mister," I said.

The saddle creaked as he shifted his weight. A half nod was his only reply.

"Something I can do for you?"

He looked up at the slowly turning wheel of the windmill and followed the frame down to where a trickle of water spilled from the pipe into the hollowed half-log trough. Overflow at the far end puddled in the mud and darkened a circle of dirt.

The rider hunched his shoulders and rolled his head around on his neck. He slid his hat off and used a shirtsleeve to wipe his forehead and across the top of his scalp. "I wonder if I could trouble you for a drink of water for me and my horse."

"Dime for you. Two bits for the animal."

One eyebrow arched, and the other squinted, plowing furrows in his forehead. His face straightened out, and he licked his lips. "That's not very neighborly of you."

"This place is a business proposition. It is not a charity," I told him, hitching my thumbs into my braces. "The woman has coffee inside if you want some. Coffee costs a dime. Free, if you buy a meal—that would be fifty cents."

He lifted a leg over the cantle and swung out of the saddle, leather groaning as he stepped down. From his pocket he fetched a half-dollar coin. I caught it out of the air.

"Not hungry," he said. Lifting the rust-smudged tin cup from the bent nail it hung on, he dipped it full and emptied it with long swallows. He clucked his tongue and tightened the rein in his hand, urging the horse forward to drink from the trough, downstream, then dipped another cupful for himself and nursed it slow as his mount buried its muzzle and sucked, the water hissing through its lips.

I flipped the half dollar up and watched it spin, caught it, and slid it into my pocket. "I will have to go inside to bring you the difference."

"Don't bother," he said as he slipped the handle of the cup back over the nail on the windmill frame. "I'll be back this way before too many days. Might be thirsty again, then."

"Likely so, seeing as this is the only good water for many a mile on this road."

He gave me another half nod, checked the cinch, untracked his horse, and stepped into the saddle, tapping the horse's belly with spurred heels to rejoin the long road across the wide valley. The man's neck swiveled this way and that as he studied the draft cattle in the corral, the penned horses, and the stock scattered in the bare pasture, watching him. He looked over the outbuildings, although they are not much to look at. He noticed the rock rim around the old well. The wagons parked beside the log building where we kept the store and roadhouse and sleeping room in the back caught his eye, as did the woman, leaning half-shadowed against the doorframe.

She disappeared into the dimness of the roadhouse, and when

I passed through the doorway I still could not see her. When my eyes adjusted to the gloom I saw her at the stove against the far wall, stirring a steaming pot of something. I fetched a bottle of warm beer from behind the store counter, scraped a chair across the rough board floor, and sat at the table. The woman banged the spoon against the top edge of the pot and turned to look at me with a question in her eyes.

"I do not know who he is," I said, after swigging off a draught of the foamy brew. "He said he would be back. You can ask him then."

The woman scrunched up her already ugly face into a hateful look. I laughed and hefted the bottle for another swallow, holding it out her way like I was toasting her good health or some such. She frowned even harder and turned back to the stove, thrashing the contents of the pot with the spoon and raising more of a ruckus at it than was needed. I emptied the last of the beer down my throat. The bottle broke into a hundred pieces when it hit the wall above the stove. My chair grated across the floor as I slid back from the table.

"Clean up that mess," I said and walked outside into sunlight. I stopped and rubbed at my clenched eyelids with a thumb and forefinger, scrubbing away the pain of the glare.

The horseback man came again in four days' time. It was along toward evening when he came across the valley, his shadow stretched out long in front of him. The shade passed over the trough, and, when the horse caught up with it, the animal dipped his head to drink but lifted it again when the reins tightened. The horse was not the same one he rode in on before.

Stepping down, the rider looked my way. He half nodded at me like before. I lifted my chin in reply, but I did not move from where I sat on the one step that led up to the roadhouse. He let the horse drink from the trough, and this time he filled the cup from the pipe. The horse drank its fill, or as close as the man would allow so the animal wouldn't sicken. The man mounted again and rode over to the building, even though it was no more than three rods' distance. He reined up where I could not see him and he could not see me, the horse's head between us, and sat there for a time. Then he clucked his tongue and touched a rein and the horse's front legs shuffled half a step to the left. The man looked down at me.

"He ain't drunk his fill yet. He'll finish up in the morning," he said.

"The hell you say! The way I figure it, you owe me two bits for what the two of you have drunk already. If you want more in the morning, you pay again."

"Your countin' ain't up to much, mister. I paid a half dollar the other day when I come through. That's a dime for me and a quarter for the horse and fifteen cents left over. The way I've got it figured, I don't owe you but twenty cents."

Two dimes hit the ground at my feet. The one shone in the sun, but I had to scratch around for the other, as it had slipped into the inch or so of dust at the bottom of the step. I blew the dust off and palmed it with the other coin. He lit off his horse and handed me a rein.

"I'll be stayin' over the night," he said. "Take care of my horse."

"I am not a hostler. Tend to your own caballo." I handed the leather back to him. "I will tell the woman to get some food ready. We have already eaten, but I suppose there will be some leftovers." I thumbed over my shoulder toward the washstand shelf nailed to the roadhouse wall, where there sat a pitcher of water and an enamel washbowl. "You can wash up there, if you are of a mind to. There is no soap. The outhouse is out back if you need it."

He came in after a bit, stepping through the doorway, then

stepping off to the side while his eyes adjusted to the low light, so as not to be silhouetted in the frame. A coal oil lantern on the table and another on the store counter were the only light in the place, and one of them would be snuffed out had the man not been there.

"Have a seat," I said and stepped into the halo of light from the lantern on the counter. "The woman has food laid out for you." Again, the half nod. In the man's vocabulary, that gesture served a mighty purpose, it appeared.

He walked around the table and pulled back a chair on the opposite side, where he could keep an eye on the door. Or maybe me. He slid the cup of coffee across the table, then the plate of stew, then the napkin wrapped around a slice of bread. The bread tumbled out into his hand when he lifted the napkin. I could see I would have to talk to the woman about not slicing it so thick. He tore off a piece of bread, chewed it, and washed it down with coffee. He lifted his backside off the seat and leaned forward across the table to reach the spoon laying there and carried it back and went to work on the stew. The man was either right hungry or thought more of the woman's cooking than I did. He wiped his mouth and dropped the napkin on the plate, wiped clean of every bit of food with the last of the bread slice.

"What've you got to drink?" he said.

"Whiskey—rye or corn. Rum. And I have bottled beer, but it is not cold."

"Pour me a shot of rye." He stood and walked over to the counter. "I'll take it here. Been sittin' on that horse all day long and need to straighten out my legs some."

He sipped the whiskey and eyed the goods on the shelf behind the counter. "Thought you said you didn't have any soap," he said, gesturing with his glass toward the four cakes of paper-wrapped soap on the shelf.

"Only what is there for sale. Be happy to sell you some, if you want."

He shook his head and sipped and kept up his study. "Quite a selection of stuff you've got, for such an out-of-the-way place."

I did not answer. The man kept looking, studying every item the light hit.

"How is it you get your goods? From what I'm told, there ain't no stagecoach on this road no more." He watched me close for a time, then looked into his glass and swirled the whiskey around the bottom and watched the film of it slide back down the sides.

"There has not been a coach on the road through here for nigh onto two years. Used to be, there were two every day—one going each way. This place was a stage station, for a fact, before I bought it when they shut down the line. They pulled up stakes when the mines in the mountains played out, or mostly did.

"We see nester wagons from time to time. But most folks heading for California take the road up north. More miles that way, but there is water. A few wagons come by, but not many anymore. Every now and again a freighter comes through on the way to those old mining towns."

"That how you get your supplies? You never said."

"You ask a lot of questions for a man who has no business asking them."

He shrugged.

I said, "Let me ask you a question. What is it you are doing away out here?"

The man took another sip of his whiskey, dribbling it out slowly like he wanted it to last. Then he said, "Got me a job carryin' letters to them mining towns. There's still a few folks lives there, and they got a right to get mail."

I nodded. "I thought that might be it. There was another man doing the same, but he has not been by for several weeks."

"That's what I was told. Said he rode out but never come back. They don't know what happened to him." He wet his tongue again with the whiskey. "You got any idea?" His eyes locked on mine like there was some unseen thing holding them there.

I shrugged. "I could not say. Maybe he got tired of it and just kept riding. Could be the Indians got him. There are not many left hereabouts, but if they catch a man out alone, they will take advantage." I looked away, but his eyes found mine again. I shrugged. "Like I said, I do not know what happened. I guess he is just gone." I lifted a rag out from under the counter and wiped a spot that did not need it. "There might be a lesson in that for you."

The last of the whiskey trickled out of the glass and down his throat. He set the glass on the counter and slid it my way. "How much do I owe you?"

I toted up in my head the price of the meal and drink, and board for his horse, and when I gave him the sum he asked if it included water for his horse and himself come morning. I added that in and told him it included filling his canteen as well as his belly.

"I reckon I can stand the cost of another whiskey," he said. "Pour it."

A splash missed the glass and wet the counter as the liquor glugged out of the bottle. I lifted the glass and wiped away the spill.

He said, "I ain't payin' for that."

I looked up and saw he was smiling. Still, I did not take the thought of it kindly.

Again, he partook of the rye as if it were the good stuff. With half of it gone, he started in to talking again.

"Where's your woman? I seen her in the doorway the other day. She shy, or something?"

I nodded toward the curtained doorway across the room. He turned to look, but all he saw was the curtain waving a bit as the woman pulled it to.

"She your wife?"

I shook my head. "Common law, I guess, maybe. Our union has not been solemnized." I shifted weight from one leg to another and leaned down to prop a forearm on the counter. "She is Paiute. Some people are offended at the notion of a white man keeping house with an Indian. She finds it best to keep out of sight."

"Well, I don't mind. She don't need to stay hid out on my account."

He swallowed off the last of the whiskey in one gulp. I guess the drink outlasted the talk. We settled up, and he asked where he could put down his bedroll. I told him there were miles and miles of opportunity just outside the door. I added there was a fire ring out in the yard where most folks camped.

Upon being stirred out of sleep in the wee hours of the morning by a forgotten yet vexing dream, I rousted the woman out early to get the fire stoked in the stove. The only sound around the place was the creaking of the windmill. The man and his horse were already gone.

CHAPTER TWO

The horses in the box canyon looked good. Not what you would call fat, but they were well fleshed, their hides slick and glistening in the sun. There was nothing to hold them in the canyon, other than good grass and spring water. But that was enough. Oh, now and again there would be one with the wanderlust, but losing the occasional horse did not bother me overmuch.

I dismounted and wrapped a bridle rein around the stub of a broken-off limb on the lone cottonwood tree standing by the spring. Before I had the cinch loosened, the old mare already stood hipshot, showing the sole of one hind hoof. Seven miles from the home place wasn't enough of a trip to tire a horse, but the mare was tired before we left and was always so. But she could make the trip out here and back with her eyes closed, and I suppose she did just that. Her plodding added a goodly amount of time to the journey, but I was damned if I would put miles on a good horse. Those, I kept only for sale. And the most of them I kept hidden away in this canyon, so as not to arouse suspicion about my having a herd this size.

The shade cast by the wall of the cabin looked inviting, and I decided to accept the invitation. The walls were the only part of the shack still standing, the flat roof having long since taken up residence inside. I suppose I could have hauled out the old shorn saplings that once served as beams, and the leftovers of the brush and limbs and dirt that had shingled the roof. Maybe, had I been inclined to kindle a fire ever and burned the debris,

I might have done so. But, to my way of thinking, that trash was as well off where it lay as anyplace else.

I brushed dust and leaves off the cut-stone step in front of the empty doorway and sat. A sandwich of thick-sliced ham and a cut of crumbly cheese showed itself as I unwound the dish towel the woman had wrapped the meal in. The bread she sliced for me wasn't nearly so generous as that carved from the loaf when she fed strangers. I would have to mention it to her.

Napping where I sat, propped against the door frame, some unremembered dream troubled me. I snapped awake, blinking away the disquiet. I stood, holding to the splintered jamb for support, and stretched the kinks out of my back. The mare snorted and shivered when I lifted the stirrup and slapped the leathers over the seat. Must have awakened her. I snugged up the cinch, then lifted my knee hard into the horse's belly. She coughed and the wind she had held to keep the girth from tightening left her in a heave. I pulled the slack out of the latigo and fixed the cinch ring prong into a hole.

On the way down the narrow valley, I checked the horses again. But, this time, the cattle got more attention. Oxen were harder to shift, but now and then I could sell a team, or maybe only one, to a traveler with weary and footsore animals. The oxen, the meat steers, and the mother cows with their calves looked to be in good shape.

The mare stopped at the canyon's mouth without being asked. I spent a few minutes watching the valley for any sign of movement. There was none. No dust hung above where the road would be, far across the sagebrush plain. I kicked the mare in the belly, and she leaned into motion. I glanced back at the canyon. I would see it again in eight days.

The woman's brothers helped me cut out the horses. The two Paiute boys made fair hands, if you did not expect any thinking on their part. We pushed twenty head of likely looking saddle stock out of the canyon and turned the herd to the north.

I gave the boys my instructions for the umpteenth time. Hard, dark eyes stared into mine, but I could not see in them any sign that my words were heard. Still, they knew where the army post was, away up on the river. They had been there before, on errands just like this one, so I figured they could and would make the delivery.

The horses were ordered by the quartermaster sergeant at the fort two weeks ago as remounts for the cavalry troopers. The sergeant was not too particular about any brands the horses might carry, unless burned with the army's own *US*. He paid a fair enough price, less than what he would have to pay elsewhere. But he paid me in government gold and asked no questions, so I did not push the man too hard on price.

Besides, what he paid was more or less straight profit.

I watched the herd until there was nothing to see but a distant haze of dust, then turned for home.

"Anybody been by on the road?"

The woman turned away from her work and shook her head. She turned back to the carcass hanging from the crossbeam of the ramada, wiped the blood off the blade of her knife against the hair below the deer's hock, and went back to whittling meat off the hind leg. The rest of the animal was picked clean; the cuts of meat stacked in a washtub. Now and then she would wave the butcher knife over the tub in a half-hearted effort to shoo off the flies. The strips of meat carved from the leg, with other slabs cut from elsewhere on the carcass, would hang in the smoke of a piñon fire. Jerky had a long shelf life in this dry country. What we couldn't sell, we'd eat.

By the time I put up the horse, the woman was done with her butchering. I was glad for the meat, but it meant extra pay for her brothers, who had flushed out the doe on the way here and brought it in. I would have to watch the woman when her brothers came by on the way home, or too much of the coming jerky would leave when they did. I watched as the woman bundled up the scraps and bones and viscera and such in the deer hide and hefted it over her shoulder. She set the bundle on the rock rim of the dry well, rolled a hold on the edge of the hide into her hands, and lifted to push the offal over the edge. Shaking the hide a time or two to rid it of clingy bits, she folded and rolled it up. Later, she'd flesh it and stake it out to dry. The hide would bring something—more, if she had saved out the deer's brains to tan it.

I spent the cool of the evening messing about in the wagon yard. With a rasp, I abraded the top of an ox-team yoke. The former owner had burned his name into it, and it would not do to leave it there. Once the man's name was erased, I rubbed soil and axle grease into the raw wood to where it blended well enough with the weathered wood around it.

That same man had put his hot iron to work on the wagon box, as well. The tailgate was branded with the family name, and he'd fire-etched "Californy bound" on the sideboards in crude letters. There was nothing to be done for it. I pulled off the bolster stakes and bows and heaved off the box and took an axe to it. It would do for stove wood. Once I'd done away with the box and sorted out the bolts and screws and other iron pieces, I hefted the tongue and pushed the running gear into a space between a wagon entire and another one stripped down.

At least the man who'd owned the wagon restricted his handiwork to writing with fire. Thankfully, he hadn't daubed the canvas wagon cover with paint. I folded it into a bundle and stored it in a shed with a stack of the same. The bows I leaned against the back wall with some others.

I called it all a day's work, hoping it would turn a profit.

Along about midmorning the next day the man carrying the

mail came back. I watched him come down the road off the pass and across the valley. He stopped a ways out and studied the place. There was no smoke from the chimney, and he could not see me from where I was in the barn, and the woman was somewhere inside the roadhouse. Far as he could see, the place may as well be abandoned. I wondered what he would do if left with that idea.

After a time, he rode on to the windmill and watered himself and his horse. He checked his cinch and remounted but looked around some more before heeling the horse into motion. He rode no farther than the old well, reining up his horse next to it. He stood on one stirrup to lean over and look down the well.

I stepped out of the barn. "You owe me thirty-five cents."

If my presence surprised him, he did not show it. Satisfied there was nothing down the well but darkness, he looked my way and gave me that half nod of his.

I walked his way. He rode toward me and turned the horse sideways to where I stood. He pulled a leather drawstring pouch from his vest pocket, fingered around inside, and handed me a two-bit coin and a dime.

"Highway robbery. That's what this is," he said.

"A man would be hard-pressed to call this road a highway anymore."

"You know, mister, me bein' on official business and all, I could likely make a case for you providin' me water as a public duty."

"You could try. I do not know as anybody would listen. Least-ways, not anyone whose opinion on the subject mattered—that being me."

We watched each other for a time, deciding if that subject had been covered. Then he started up another discussion.

"Any water in that well yonder?"

"No. They say it never was much good. Goes down near sixty

feet, but never drew much water. Went bone dry when they drilled the hole for the wind pump."

"It sure as hell stinks."

"That it does. Me and the woman dump trash down there now. Fact is, she threw what was left of a nice young muley doe down that well just yesterday."

He looked away toward the well as if imagining the rotting gut and bone pile in its depths, then turned back to me and only stared.

I said, "I throw down a bucket of lime now and then, and shovel in some dirt. Along about the time my grandkids have grandkids, the hole might be filled right up. If I were to have any grandkids, that is. Having no offspring just now, the prospect seems unlikely."

For another few minutes that seemed longer, he studied the wagon yard, the barn and outbuildings, the pens and corrals, and the livestock. He looked to the roadhouse in time to catch the woman closing the door.

And then, without another word, he gave me that half nod of his and rode away.

The boys came by a few days later. The one hefted the saddlebags with the gold onto the table in front of me. I swallowed off the last of the coffee in my enameled mug and tossed it in the direction of the washtub. The coin sack landed with a dull jingle when I pawed it out of the saddlebag and onto the tabletop. I picked it up to test its weight. Counting would come later. For now, I was satisfied that the army had satisfied its debt.

I unwound the tie string from the mouth of the money sack and pulled out a pair of gold coins. The boys sat opposite me. I slid a coin toward each of them. Their eyes never left mine.

"It is not enough."

The one who spoke, the younger of the two, stood. With the palms of his hands on the table, he leaned toward me.

My eyes followed his as he rose. "Same as always," I told him.

The brother still on his chair grabbed the sash around the waist of the other and pulled him back to his seat. He said, "There is also the matter of the deer."

I laughed. "The deer. The woman will send you out of here with more meat than that skinny doe was worth."

He shrugged. "There was much parlaying with the officer at the fort. He was not pleased with the horses you sent. It took much talk to collect the agreed-upon price."

With a snort, I said, "There was nothing wrong with any of those horses. You are lying."

The first brother again jumped out of this seat and slapped a hand to the tabletop. But, this time, the other hand held a knife of the kind called Arkansas Toothpick.

His older brother tugged at this sash to sit him down, but he ignored it. I rose slowly from my chair, my eyes locked on his. I stood head and shoulders taller than the Paiute boy. When I leaned toward him with my fists on the table, I saw a tic in his left eyelid, and he leaned back ever so slightly.

"Put the knife down," I said.

He said nothing. His brother grabbed his wrist and gripped it hard, and the knife clattered to the table. A flash of courage prompted the boy to lean further into me. His breath smelled of stale tobacco and the rotting food between his teeth. "You are a cheat!" he hissed.

His dark eyes widened until white showed all around. He sucked in his breath, stood up straight, and looked down to see the upright handle of the knife trembling and the blade pinning his hand to the table.

I must give the boy credit. He did not cry out. He fell onto his chair, staring at the blood seeping onto the tabletop from beneath his hand. His breathing quickened. His brother again grabbed his wrist and held it to the table, then stood and grasped the knife handle and jerked it upward and out of the boy's hand. Then he, too, sat.

"You had no need to do that," he said, dark eyes flashing beneath furrowed brow.

I shrugged.

"He meant no harm."

"He pulled a knife on me. Seems harmful, to my way of thinking."

The boy sat, the wrist of the punctured hand in the white-knuckled grip of the other. Blood dripped into his lap. He stared, still wide eyed, at the oozing hole.

My chair scraped against the floor as I hung a bootheel over a rail and pushed it out of the way. I picked up the money sack, twisted the mouth, and wrapped the tie string. "You boys take your money and get the hell out of here. The woman will fix you up with some food to go with you."

The older brother stood. "We will not be coming back here."

I laughed, but there was no mirth in it. "Like hell. That gold is worth more to you all than that pinprick." I started for the sleeping room to roust out the woman. Before pulling the curtain closed, I said, "I will send for you boys next time I need you."

CHAPTER THREE

Cooking is not a thing I enjoy. And, truth be told, I am no good at it. Still, I stood at the stove scraping the black crust of a batch of cornbread off the bottom of the pan. The woman huddled in the corner wrapped in a blanket, quivering. Since her brothers left, she had been shirking her work. As yet, my encouragement had not taken effect despite the festering welts on her back and legs.

Give it time. I am nothing if not a patient man.

I dipped some water into the pan and set it on the stove. The warmth and wet may well loosen the cornbread cinders, given time. As I said, I am a patient man.

I saw the riders coming on my way out to the windmill to refill the kitchen bucket. They came from the west. Three of them. They did not hurry, their mounts lumbering along as if jaded.

Water sloshed over the rim of the bucket as I hefted it onto the shelf, dripping to a puddle on the floor. It was no big thing. But, somehow, it burned a few more inches off my fuse. I kicked the woman and lifted her by the hair. "Company coming. There better be something for them to eat when they get here, or I will know the reason why." I landed a swift kick on her ample backside and left her to her labors.

The riders were near enough now that the reason for the slow pace of their arrival revealed itself. The man on the left rode a black horse, the knurl of its ribcage pronounced. You could hang your hat on a hip bone. It walked with its head low, as did the dun pony under the man on the right. I say pony, owing to the horse's size—likely a mustang, it could not have stood thirteen hands on its tiptoes. The mane was long and tangled, hanging well below the neck, and the tail looked to be trimmed only by the rubbing of the ground over which it dragged. Unshod, the dun's hooves were crumbled and cracked at the rims.

The man in the middle of the trio looked to be the best mounted of the bunch. He rode a mule, brown as plug tobacco and well fleshed, at least when measured against the animals flanking it. The mule carried its head high, moving it from side to side with each step. The long ears were on swivels, continually turning and twisting, and tilting to every angle. As the mule drew closer, I could see it lacked soundness despite my earlier impression—both shoulders were sweenied. Hard work under harness, rather than a saddle, must have been the mule's accustomed duty, causing the atrophied muscles.

I stood between the riders and the trough when they reined up. Their faces were in shadow cast by the brims of their hats, but I could see enough to believe the rider on the dun was Mexican, the other two, white men.

"We'll be wantin' to water these horses," the man on the black said.

"The mule, too," said its rider.

I smiled. "You are welcome to all the water you and your animals can drink. Two bits apiece for the mounts, a dime from each of you."

The men looked at each other, then at me. The man on the black spoke again.

"We come a long way, mister. These horses is thirsty."

"And the mule."

"Like I said, there is plenty of water."

The man dismounted from the black and unhitched the flap of his saddlebag. He rummaged around and drew out a cloth bag and shook it. "You can see from the jingle we got money to pay—even if it don't seem right. You tote it up, and we'll pay. If you got food, we'll pay for that, too."

"And a drink of somethin' better'n water," said the man on the mule.

I stood aside and with a sweep of my arm toward the trough, invited them to partake. "Come on in when you are finished. There is a washstand by the door if you care to use it. You will find water and a rag to towel off with, but no soap."

Inside, the woman was at the stove where she belonged, stirring desiccated vegetables into a soup pot. I had left chunks of jerked deer meat soaking in the pot since yesterday night and I figured, rightly so, that it had made the meat and broth for the mix. Since there would be no cornbread or biscuits, a loaf of sourdough bread sat on the sideboard.

"Mind how you slice that bread," I said. "Don't be cutting it so thick."

The woman gave no sign she even heard what I said, but I knew she did.

I heard splashing in the washbasin outside, and, soon after, the men came in. They walked to the center of the room and stopped to get their bearings. The store counter and shelves got a look, and they gave the woman the once over. She kept her back to the room, stirring the soup.

"We have soup and bread. Soup will be ready soon. Fifty cents for the meal. Coffee comes with it."

"Mighty steep for a dish of hot water," the man who rode the black horse said.

"Do not worry yourselves. There is plenty of meat floating in that soup. Vegetables, too."

"Damn well better be, at prices like you charge."

The man who rode the mule said, "What you got to drink? That water of yours didn't nowhere near cut the dust in my gullet."

"Whiskey. Rye or corn. Rum. Bottled beer, but it is not cold."

They sat at the table, two of them where they could watch the door. The Mexican sat opposite, watching the woman at the stove.

"Bring us a bottle of that corn liquor. Three glasses."

"What kind of place is this?" the mule man said as I dealt out the glasses and poured them full.

"It was built as a stage station. Home station, it was, which accounts for the barn and outbuildings and pens. I bought the place after the express company pulled out."

The black-horse man swallowed off his whiskey in one long gulp. He slammed the glass to the tabletop and wrinkled up his face and shook his head. Once he caught his breath, he refilled his glass and said, "Can't be many people comin' this way, what with the mines yonder way all but gone. We just cut the population there by three."

I answered from behind the counter as I lit the wicks on a pair of coal oil lamps. "That is true enough. But we manage to keep our hand in." I carried one of the lamps to the table. "You gentlemen are coming from the mines, then?"

"We are. Not much work there these days. Towns is pretty much gone save a few hangers-on."

"If you do not mind my saying so, those horses of yours are in sorry shape."

The men laughed. "Hell, mister, them was about the only mounts for sale. Anything worth strappin' a saddle to can't be bought at any price."

I cleared my throat. "That mule looks to have been worked hard in the harness. Sweeney on both shoulders."

The mule rider said, "Spent more time underground in them

mines than me, that mule did. Pullin' ore cars. He's still plenty strong, though."

"I see where he moves his head and ears around in an unusual way."

The man who rode the black horse laughed and punched the mule man on the shoulder. "That ol' mule is near blind as a bat. Can't see hardly a damn thing. But if we keep 'im in the middle, he finds his way all right."

The mule man swatted at him, knocking his hat askew. "You just shut up about my mule. That sonofabitch will still be walkin' long after that bag of bones you're on falls dead in the road." He paused for a swallow of liquor. "Besides, even comin' down a trail on his own, he finds his way. A mite slow, but sure-footed as a cat."

I let the men drink for a while. "If you gentlemen are of a mind to, I could make you a good deal on fresh mounts."

They thought on it for a time and whispered among themselves. The black-horse man said, "I don't know. We'll talk come the mornin'." He drank more whiskey. "Hey! You! Woman! That soup ready? My stomach thinks my throat's been cut!"

The woman turned away from the bread loaf she was slicing and gave the man a look that would have curled his hair had he not been wearing a hat. As it was, he could not hold her stare. He picked up the bottle to fill his glass. I swear I saw a tremble in his hand.

In another few minutes—a few more than necessary, I would say—the woman carried soup plates to the table and dropped them in front of the men with no concern for splash of hot liquid. After tossing a woven basket full of sliced bread on the table, she heavy-footed her way through the curtain to our sleeping quarters and pulled it shut behind her.

"Would you all care for any coffee?" I said.

"Sure," the mule man said. "Set us up all around."

"And bring us another bottle of that whiskey," said the black-horse man.

I kept their plates and mugs full, seething somewhat at the absence of the woman, but not caring over much. "Where is it you are going, if I might ask—meaning no offense."

"Home," the mule man said around a mouthful of bread.

"Where is home?"

"Springfield, Illinois, for me."

The man who rode the black horse said he was bound for Virginia.

"And you," I said with a nod toward the Mexican, who had yet to say a word other than whispering with his companions. "Will you be returning to Mexico?"

"No, no," he said with a waggle of his finger. "*No soy Mexicano.* I am Chileno. I go home to Chile."

I shrugged. "Cheelay, huh? Oh, well—your kind are all Mexicans to me."

"No. Chileno," he said and turned back to his soup.

When the men finished the meal, I gathered the soup plates and spoons and mugs and stacked them on the sideboard for the woman to deal with.

The mule man sat back and belched. He reached in a shirt pocket and came back with a toothpick and put it to work. "You got a deck of cards around here?"

I fetched a pack from under the counter and carried it to the table, along with a rack of chips.

"How much?" the black-horse man said.

"What?"

"What's the charge for the use of the cards?"

The men laughed at the dirty look I gave him.

"Bring us another bottle," the mule man said. "I do believe it's gettin' to where I can almost stand the taste."

The black-horse man said, "You got any tobaccer?"

"Yes. Chewing and smoking. What is your pleasure?"

"Bring me a pouch of smoking tobaccer. And a bible."

With the tobacco and rolling papers and more whiskey delivered, I sat at the counter. The hours stretched long, watching the men play cards and drink whiskey. But I was content to sit as long as their money was good. They squabbled occasionally. Laughed. Traded insults and told obscene stories. The Mexican—the Chileno—leaned toward the mule man and whispered something. The mule man threw back his head and laughed, then pounded the Chileno on the back.

"Say there, mister," he said to me in a raised voice. "That woman back there for sale?"

"No. I suppose I could rent her out, though. It would not be the first time."

"How much?"

After lengthy negotiations, during which I refused to yield on my price, the man who rode the black horse staggered across the floor and pushed through the curtain. I carried another bottle of whiskey to the table and gathered the empties.

"This one is on the house."

By the time the black-horse man came back, the other two were fighting to keep their eyes open. But the Chileno struggled to his feet and found his way through the curtain after batting at it a time or two.

The black-horse man poured a glass full and drank it down in one swallow. "What's the matter with that woman?"

"What do you mean?"

"Well, she never talked. Never said a word."

"She does not have much to say, I suppose."

He emptied his glass again. "When I woke her up, she tried to say somethin' but nothin' came out—like the words was just wallerin' around in her mouth. Nothin' but a lot of blubberin'."

I said nothing for a time, but he was insistent. "She has no tongue."

He looked as if I was speaking in tongues, in some language he could not make sense of. "No tongue?" he finally said. "Why the hell not?"

I shrugged. "It was cut from her mouth."

"Cut? Clean out?"

I nodded. He again emptied his glass, then slouched in his chair looking troubled. After a few minutes, his chin landed on his chest, his eyelids shuttered, and his every breath rattled in his throat. The Chileno shuffled his way back to the table, shook the mule man awake. The mule man pushed himself upright but sat back down. The Chileno sat, picked up a glass and studied its contents, then drank them down. He folded his arms on the tabletop, laid his head on their pillow, and closed his eyes.

"I'm sick," the mule man said. He sat in the chair unsteady, weaving slowly in search of equilibrium.

I helped him up. "Come along. I'll help you outside. I'll not have you being sick on my floor." I slung his arm around my shoulder and half carried, half dragged him out the door. We stumbled our way to the old well, and I leaned him over the stone wall and listened to him heave as I caught my breath. When he stood up, propped on his arms atop the rim of the wall, I reached my arm around and with the woman's butcher knife sliced deep across his throat. Blood gushed out, following the track of the vomit down the well. I pushed him over the wall and listened as he fell, scraping the wall now and then until bottoming out with a thunk that echoed up the well shaft.

The mule man's friends shared his fate. Except both of them held their stomachs.

Dancing flicker of flames reflected on the ceiling. The murmur of voices in the dark. A woman sobbing. The boy turned in the bed and sat, legs dangling over the side, toes feeling about on the floor for carpet slippers. His eyes opened and closed in turn, and his yet-dormant mind struggled free of sleep.

At the window, he watched below as men milled about in the dooryard, the blaze of upheld torches illuminating then obscuring upturned faces. His mother sat on the front steps, head hung low and shoulders convulsing. Her wrists bound with twine laced through the balusters of the porch rail. The boy's father looked to be looking down on those assembled as he swayed slowly from the loop in a rope thrown over a limb of the sycamore tree, hands corded at the small of his back.

Through heavy-lidded eyes the boy looked from face to face. The barber. The man who owned the clothing store. The farm implement salesman. The ticket agent at the train station. The deacon at the church who taught him Sunday school. The druggist. Other faces he recognized but did not know. Other faces strange to him. The swelled and distorted and blackened face of his father.

The men of the town felt hard done by the boy's father. He owned the bank. The bank failed. And, with it, the promise of tomorrow.

The boy sat down on the bed.

CHAPTER FOUR

You can be certain I checked the men's pockets for valuables before sending them down the well. I found little of worth, save a handful of gold coins stitched into the shafts of the Chileno's boots. Like the man on the black horse, the other two had carried pouches of money in their saddlebags. Not bad pay, for one night's work.

Their clothing was in such a state of disrepair as to be worthless. I burned it. I saved out the bridle bits and dumped the remaining horse furniture down the well. The saddle stock I treated to one last drink of water, and, in the evening, I saddled my old mare and led the haltered mule across the plain and over the saddleback pass. The horses followed. About a mile beyond the summit I cut into a shallow side canyon, took my halter from the mule, and left the worthless mounts to fend for themselves.

As travelers on the road often do, I stopped atop the pass and studied the valley below. Things looked different from up here. The windmill cast a long shadow, and I imagined I could hear the sluggish squeak of the fan. The animals were but shifting specks in their pens. The buildings looked clean and orderly, if humble. The low rock wall around the old well was visible if one knew where to look. It was easy to imagine the relief a traveler would feel upon seeing the place, after crossing many an empty mile on the road.

The sun was down by the time I got home. I tended to the

old mare, then in the twilight shoveled up a wheelbarrow load from an aged manure pile behind the barn, shoveled it into the well, and followed it with another.

For days to come there were no travelers on the road save the man who carried the mail. He passed going west and, days later, going east. He stopped only for water and complained at the cost. As always, he was attentive to his surroundings. As always, there was little to hold his interest. I saw to it. A curious man like him needed watching.

The old mare and I visited the box canyon to check the stock. I rode through the scattered animals. Then again. While I could not put an exact number to it, I believed myself to be short six or eight horses. The loss of beef steers was easier to tally. There were eleven grazing in the canyon when last I came. Now, there were nine.

The woman stood watching in the doorway of the roadhouse when I rode in. After putting up the mare, I found her picking trash out of a spread of dry beans on the table. The chair tipped over backward from the force of my backhand blow. The bowl clattered, and the beans rattled across the floor. She looked up at me in pain and wonder and put a hand to her reddening cheek.

"Those brothers of yours have robbed me."

She sat up, legs spraddled, and slowly shook her head, staring at me with some admixture of puzzlement, misery, and hatred.

"Right now, those damned blanket-ass Indians in your village are feasting on my beef, unless I miss my guess. And your useless brothers are riding my horses—if they have not sold them off already."

The woman rolled to her knees and, bracing herself against the table edge, rose to her feet. She fetched the broom and dustpan from the corner and swept up the beans from the floor and dumped them back onto the tabletop, picked up the bowl, lifted the chair upright, then sat down and went back to her work cleaning the beans.

The freighter came by the next week. He was one I had not seen before. The Murphy wagon waddled down the grade from the pass and across the flat, drawn by a single team under yoke, with another team tied to the back. One of those hobbled along with a severe limp.

He drifted off the road into the yard and pulled up between the roadhouse and windmill. "I could use some water for these cattle," he said.

"Take all you need. Two bits a head."

"Two bits? That's a steep price for something that don't cost you nothing."

"That wind pump did not come cheap. And there is the money to maintain it."

The freighter wore bibbed overalls and a woven straw hat of a style not often seen in these parts. A big man, he was, with a big head. He had a big face, with the features all squished into the middle. Studying him, I believed I could, with the palm of my hand, cover eyebrows to lower lip.

He licked his lips, snakelike. "That mill didn't cost you anything. Overland stage line drilled that well and put up the mill. I know, for I freighted it in here." He nodded in the direction of the road. "I hauled on this road regular-like, back then."

"That is as it may be. Concerning the windmill, I mean. But I paid for this place whole, it included. So you cannot rightly say it cost me nothing."

The freighter didn't answer. He went about the business of unhitching the team and leading them still yoked to the trough. He then untied the other pair from the tailgate and led them to drink.

"That ox's foot doesn't look so good," I said.

"Picked up a stob of wood on the road a few miles back. Slipped right up between the shoes and into the meat. Damndest thing I ever seen in all my years handling cattle." He lifted the tin cup from its peg on the windmill frame and dipped it full from the trough.

"That is a dime you are holding there," I said.

He drank down the cup, his eyes over the rim never leaving mine. When he finished, he waved the cup in the direction of a cow pen. "I suppose there's a similar amount of larceny in the price of them oxen in yonder yard."

Walking among the oxen in the corral, he looked them in the eye, looked in their mouths, looked them over head to tail. He rubbed their necks where the yoke carried, lifted their feet. He waved his arms and hooted at them to test their disposition. He found what he thought a match for the healthy ox left in his second team, clamped on a nose lead as it had no ring, and led it out of the pen.

"I'll yoke it up," he said. "See how it handles."

The freighter lifted the yoke from the wagon and laid it across the team. With practiced rapidity, he fitted the bows and keys. With goad and whip and voice commands, he walked the team around the yard, circling the wagon, the old well, the windmill, *gee*ing them to the right and *haw*ing them to the left. He *whoa*ed up near where I sat on the stone step, and we discussed price.

The lame ox had no trade value, I told him. It may not ever recover from an injury of that kind. He disagreed. I pointed out that I had no need for a crippled ox—or any kind of deal, for that matter. He was welcome to move on down the road if he did not like my terms. We finally agreed on a price that was not to his liking, but he was in a fix.

"I've not the cash in hand," he said. "My money is tied up in the goods on the wagon. You'll be paid when I come back this way from what's left of those mining towns in yonder mountains."

"Like hell. How am I to know you will not just keep on going on to California, or wherever?"

"Look, mister. You've got me over a barrel. All I can give you is my word that I'll come back on this road. With any luck, with a load of ore. Empty, if it comes to it. But I'll have your money."

I studied on it for a minute or two. Or, let him think so. "What have you got on that wagon?"

He told me that most of the goods on board were on order. But he parted with some bacon sides and hams, flour, beans, whiskey, a sack of wheat and one of oats, and a box of rifle shells. Enough to cover the cost of the ox. And then some. We then talked about his lame ox, and I agreed to keep it fed and watered while we waited to see if it would heal. Any money changing hands on the deal would be determined later.

I watched him nail shoes on his new ox and reset the shoes on one of the wheelers and get ready to leave. As he was latching the tailgate on the Murphy wagon, the man who carried the mail came by. Still in the saddle, he gave me that half nod and flipped a quarter then a dime my way. I caught them out of the air in turn and walked away.

From inside the roadhouse I watched the two of them standing by the water trough talking. From time to time the freighter looked somewhere or other on the place in response to something or other the man said. The horseback man stepped into the stirrup and gave the freighter that half nod of his. He turned and looked at me standing in the doorway, then heeled his horse into motion. The freighter cracked his whip over the lead team, and the four oxen leaned into the yokes and set out. The freighter walked along beside, watching me watching him as he took to the road.

★　★　★　★　★

The woman was nowhere to be seen when I woke up, my mind uneasy from some passing phantasm of the night. The coffee pot was full and wisping steam on the stove. In the warming oven was a skillet with scrambled eggs and a few slices of bacon. On the table, covered with a dish towel, sat a basket with a half-dozen biscuits. How she stirred up the grub without making enough noise to wake me was a caution. On the other hand, I had taken a glass of rum the night before. Unaccustomed as I was to strong spirits, that alone may have been responsible for my unsound but long and late sleep.

Hammering from out back somewhere stirred me from my reverie as I sat nursing a second mug of coffee after I ate. I hitched up my braces and went outside to greet the day—a ceremony the sun had already undertaken, hours earlier. Wandering out behind the roadhouse, I found the woman flailing away with a hammer, nailing a board along the bottom of the side of the henhouse. The chickens were out in the run, huddled in the corner and cackling at the upset to their routine.

A lard pail piled full of eggs sat on the ground next to where the woman worked, beside the bucket she used to haul water to the chickens, and a can of nails. She started when I asked what the hell she was doing. She stood and pointed to a scratched-out place in the dirt next to the henhouse wall.

"Fox, most likely," I said. "Coyote, maybe. But I doubt it. One of those little desert foxes, looks like."

I took the hammer from her and pried off the board she had been pounding on off the wall. "Fetch me a shovel."

When she came back, I chopped with the shovel blade against the wall, cutting into the earth for a good ways along the wall. Then, I shoveled the cut into a narrow trench. I fetched an old sideboard off a wagon from a pile of scrap lumber, dropped it edge down into the slit and worked it back and forth until it leveled out, then took the hammer and nailed it to the wall with rusty and bent scavenged nails.

"That will keep him out." I handed her the shovel. "Fill in that trench and put these tools away." I sat on a nail keg in the shade of the wall and sponged the sweat off my forehead and neck with a handkerchief. By the time she finished the work, the chickens had calmed down and strutted around the pen clucking and scratching around for something to eat.

The old man, the woman's uncle, came as she packed down the last shovelful and stood to wipe her brow. I had not heard him come. When I saw her smile, I turned to see what she saw. He came around the corner of the roadhouse leading his horse. He stopped and studied her work and said something in their gibberish that passes for language. She nodded and made some hand signs, and he spoke to her again.

He turned to me. "It will come back. Sooner or later, that fox will find a way in."

I looked at the woman. "Maybe you ought to sit up tonight and shoot the little varmint." She looked perplexed, never having fired a gun to my knowledge. I said, "We can trap him, perhaps." I asked the old man if he knew how to trap a fox.

"If you have a trap, I will catch him."

We rummaged around in a shed where I had seen some old traps. He pawed through the tangle of them in the barrel. Dragging one up by the chain, he held it up and looked it over as it twisted slowly. "This is number four trap. Smallest you have. It is good for coyote. Or bobcat. For fox, number two is best. But this will do."

The trap was tarnished with rust, but not so much as to keep it from working. The old man flexed the spring and the jaws to make sure. He said that for normal trapping, the trap must be boiled until nearly black, and waxed. Care would be taken when building a set to keep man smell away. But this fox, he said, was already amongst human things so it would not matter if the trap and the set smelled of man.

Toward nightfall, he shoveled out a hole perpendicular to and close to the henhouse wall, near where the woman showed the fox had been digging. He kept digging until the hole was an inch or so deeper than the trap was tall when set. He compressed the spring, opened the jaws, and slipped the trigger into the dog on the pan. Next came a piece of paper torn from an old newspaper to cover the pan so dirt wouldn't get under it when he filled the hole and keep it from springing the trap. Then he sifted in dirt slowly to fill the hole. He left a depression above the pan. After spiking down the ring at the end of the chain, he buried that and the spring.

The old man raised upright on his knees and jabbered something at the woman. She went around the house and came back with two eggs. He broke one into the depression over the pan, sifted a little dirt over it, then cracked open the other and let it drop, shell and all, on top. He stood and brushed the dust off his hands, then his knees.

"We will see," he said and started for the roadhouse.

CHAPTER FIVE

They call them leg-hold traps. That trap the old man set surely took ahold of that fox's leg. Grabbed onto his head and neck, too. Damn near pinched them all off. The woman found the varmint dead when she went out in the morning to gather the eggs and feed and water the chickens. She skinned out the fox and nailed the hide to the henhouse wall. Sort of a warning to others of its kind, I suppose.

The old man hung around the place for four or five days, sleeping on my floor, eating at my table, warming himself at my fire, and drinking my water. At least it was not whiskey. He talked to the woman, mostly outside my hearing. I would not have known what he was saying anyway, what with him speaking that incomprehensible Paiute gibberish. She blabbered back at him now and then, but even he could not make sense of her attempts to talk. The woman fluttered her hands around making hand signs, but who knows how much of that made sense to the old man.

In the dark hours of a morning whilst lying abed, having been awakened from the unpleasantness of dreams, I felt the woman ease out from under the quilt and through the curtain. I followed.

In the dim cast of a hooded lantern, I watched the old man stuffing canned and sacked and boxed goods off the store shelves into a burlap bag. The woman pulled a blanket bundle from behind the cold stove. I reckoned it to contain what clothes and trifles she considered her own.

"What the hell is going on here?"

The pair of them froze, as if standing still as statues they might render themselves unseen in the faint light.

"So this is what all the jabbering has been about. Why you came here in the first place, old man. You have been trying to talk the woman into going back to live in those hovels you call houses in that village of yours."

The old man stood upright. The woman turned a half circle, looked at me with eyes I knew would be afire if only I could see them, her parcel coming unbound as it eased to the floor. The old man lifted the bag and set it atop the counter so gently the goods inside made no sound beyond a shuffle.

The woman's upraised arm deflected the sweep of my backhand. Still, the force was enough to take her to the floor. She curled up on her side with arms wrapped around her head. Bent over, I snatched at her hands and arms, slapping at her face and punching at her shoulder and ribs. Gasping for air, I stood and landed a kick in the small of her back.

The old man stood there, not three feet away, arm extended, hand grasping the antique Green River knife he always carried in a sheath at his side. The point snaked back and forth and trembled in the old man's grip. Had he been twenty, even ten, years younger, I might have worried at the threat.

It took two or three convulsions of breath to get enough wind to speak. "You had best put that knife back where it belongs. Or I will take it from you and stick it in your eye."

He thought it over. His arm dropped to his side. He raised it again and slipped the blade into its sheath. The woman rolled to her hands and knees and crawled away. The sole of my bare foot, planted in her backside, pushed her along. She lost balance, her face scraping the floor as her arms collapsed.

The old man's shirtfront and collar tightened when I took a

twist of it in my hand. I lifted him off the floor and shook his wasted shell like a coyote with a caught prairie dog. His heels dragged as I strode across the floor, opened the door, and flung him outside.

"You get the hell out of here, old man. And do not come back. If you do, you will never leave this place again, for you will die here."

By now, a pale ribbon of the coming day showed above the saddleback pass and the mountains that framed it. There would be no more sleep this day. I retreated behind the curtain to dress, then went out to the backhouse. The woman stood at the stove slicing bacon into a skillet when I returned. I dragged a chair out from under the table and sat. She did not turn to look at me. Nor did her eyes meet mine when she slid a mug of coffee in front of me. I watched her at her work. There would be no need to speak further of the night's unfortunate events.

The morning hours passed. I tended to the stock, and the day warmed. From atop the windmill, oil can in hand, I watched the man who carried the mail coming from the west. He veered off the road and stopped by the old well, standing in the stirrup and leaning over to stare into the darkness of the hole.

I stepped off the windmill frame as he arrived at the water trough. He gave me that half nod and dismounted. He dipped himself a cupful of water, then another, then led the horse to drink. He watched me wipe my hands clean with a rag, then passed me the price of the water.

"You keep looking in that old well as if you will find it full of water one of these days."

Again, the half nod.

"Well, was I you, I would not worry about it. Even if it was to start drawing water, that water would be mine. And you would still have to pay for it. More, even, if I had to lift it out of there by the bucketful."

"I keep thinkin' there's somethin' about that old well. Seems a shame to dump trash down it."

"Why is that?"

"Hell of a lot of work went into diggin' that hole. Can't imagine doin' all that with a shovel."

"I would not want to do it," I said. "Enough work for me just filling it back up."

He took the tin up off the nail and held it under the trickle at the end of the pipe and watched it fill. "I wonder if that well water was as good as this," he said and drank it down.

"You are many a year too late in asking that question. If you want an answer, that is."

The horse lifted its head, water dripping from its muzzle.

"You recall that freighter came by here?"

I nodded.

"He'll be comin' along. Got him a load of ore. Part of a load, anyway. Might be the last to come out of them mines. I left a day ahead of him. You'll likely see him tomorrow, maybe the day after."

"I hope he is happy with that ox he traded for. He complained enough about it when he bought it."

The man shrugged. "Got any cooked food in there?" he said with a nod toward the roadhouse building.

"Likely so. I know there is a pot of beans on the stove. Maybe biscuits. Could be cornbread. A bread loaf, if not."

"Sounds good."

I set off ahead of him. He swung into the saddle and rode the short distance, looped a bridle rein around the hitch rail, and loosened the cinch. I heard him splashing around in the washbowl while I dished up his beans. The woman watched from the doorway into the bedroom. He came in and saw her, and she looked at him. If he noticed the discolored skin on her face, he gave no sign. She drew the curtain closed.

"Got fresh cornbread here," I told him. "This morning's biscuits if you would rather."

He said the cornbread sounded good, and I cut him out a square from the pan the woman had left cooling on the sideboard. "There is honey if you want it." He nodded, in his usual way.

Two bowls of beans, another slab of cornbread, and two cups of coffee later, he pushed back from the table.

"Compliments to the cook," he said, glancing toward the curtained doorway. "Mighty fine cornbread."

He dropped a half dollar coin on the table and left.

The information about the freighter proved right. He came by late the next day. I sat on the stone step and watched him come, expecting to listen to his complaints about paying to water his oxen. But he did not stop. As he drove by, perched on the seat rather than walking, he touched a finger to the brim of his straw hat and smiled. I could see he had extra water barrels strapped to the side of the wagon. I watched him cross the sagebrush plain and climb the slant up to the pass. He did not even stop to check on the lame ox I was keeping for him.

That ox I sold him looked to be pulling his share of the load just fine.

The woman's brothers showed up late one afternoon a week or so later. They rode in looking stone faced, as usual. I watched over the rim of a coffee mug as they approached the step where I sat. The boys separated and stopped their horses some ten feet apart and ten feet away so I could not watch them both at once.

"I did not believe you when you said you would not come back here," I said. "Looks like I was right. What is it you want?" The boys only stared.

By and by the older one spoke. "We have come for our sister."

I swallowed a sip of coffee, examined the grounds suspended

in the remaining liquid, and tossed off the dregs into the dooryard dust.

"That looks like one of my horses you are on," I said to the younger one. He flinched, but his dark eyes betrayed nothing, nor did his face. "I saw where someone had been out to the canyon. Figured it would be the two of you."

The boy looked to his brother for an answer and so did I. He said nothing.

"How long did it take your people to eat those two beeves you stole?"

We sat in silence for a time.

"Well, you might as well light down off those horses and come on inside."

They followed me inside after hitching the horses to the rail. I refilled my coffee mug and sat at the table. The boys sat opposite. The younger one had not healed altogether, the scabbed-over hole still showing on the back of his hand. He saw me looking and covered the wound with the fingers of his other hand.

"Hungry?"

They looked to one another, then nodded.

"Woman!"

It took a moment for her to brush aside the curtain and step into the main room. She saw her brothers, and her face broke into a smile that soon turned to a look of fear and pleading.

"Quit your gawking and get in here and fix these boys something to eat. They have had a long ride on this fool's errand of theirs."

The woman shoved a few sticks of wood into the stove, then spooned some grease into a skillet. While it heated up, she lifted a dishtowel covering a hambone with some meat still on it and carved off several slices. She stirred the beans in the pot and while the meat sizzled carried each boy a mug of coffee.

I watched the brothers eat and waited for the first frantic frenzy to pass. With the edge off their hunger, they settled into more methodical cutting and forking, chewing and swallowing.

"You go on now," I said to the woman. "Me and the boys are about to have us a talk."

She looked at me. Looked at the boys. Looked at me again, working her mouth as if she had something to say, her eyes filling.

"Go on now!"

The woman walked away, head down, wringing her hands.

They had stopped chewing, and the older one's fork hung in the air halfway to his mouth. In a moment they turned their attention back to the food. By now the sun had fallen, and the room was growing dark. I lit a lantern and set it on the table. I looked at the brothers.

"I believe I made it clear to the old man that the woman was not going anywhere."

The younger boy pushed his plate away. "You beat her."

I laughed. "So what? Your Indian men beat their women."

The older boy said, "There is discipline. And then there is cruelty."

"You mete out discipline your way, and I will do so my own way. It is none of your business." The youngster fixed his gaze on me through slitted eyes but said nothing. I looked to the older boy. I let the silence stew for a time.

"Now, we should talk about the stock you stole."

They said nothing.

"No sense denying it. I know that one horse hitched to the rail out there came out of the canyon. And there is no question that two steers are missing. And other horses."

They said nothing. I stood and refilled my coffee mug. I hoisted the pot in their direction in invitation, and they nodded.

"You boys taken to drinking whiskey?" I said as I filled their mugs. They looked at each other and shook their heads. "Well, you steal like grown men. I guess you can drink like grown men. I will put a little something in that coffee for you. See how you like it."

From under the store counter I fetched a pocket flask. It was not filled with whiskey as one would expect. Rather, it contained laudanum collected from medicine bottles from the stores of emigrant wagons that came by. I poured a sizable splash into each of the boys' mugs. "It will taste like hell. At first. You will get used to it. Hell, you might even develop a taste for it. Plenty of men do—especially you Indians."

The boys clabbered up on tasting the doped coffee. But I urged them on with a few mild insults, and they kept at it until their mugs were dry.

"More?" I said, hoisting the flask.

They said no. The younger boy said, "Why are you not drinking?"

"Oh, I do not partake. Not much. On occasion I will have a drink or two. But it upsets my sleep. This stuff," I said, shaking the flask, "I never touch this stuff."

The boys sat watching each other and watching me as the opium took effect. They did not speak and looked somewhat troubled by what they were feeling. Soon enough, they nodded off. Whether the dose was strong enough to kill or not, I did not care. The boys were immobilized, and that would suit my purpose well enough.

I shouldered each brother in turn and carried them out to the well. A stroke of the knife assured their demise before going over the rock rim wall.

Hanging is the usual penalty for horse thieves. My way was quicker. And, one would be hard pressed to find a tree of a suitable size among the cedars and piñon pines that stippled the slopes in this country.

I penned the horses they rode in on in a corral behind the barn where the woman would be unlikely to see them. I would convey the animals to the box canyon at first opportunity.

The next morning, the woman cleaned up the supper mess left for her. If she wondered where her brothers had gone, there was no sign of it.

But, given her quiet way, you never knew for certain.

CHAPTER SIX

Voices. The sound of distant voices. At first, I thought it a dream. The beginning of yet another ephemeral haunting in the night. But my eyes were open. From the faint twilight in the room I knew it to be close, but not too close, to morning. And I realized the voices were real. Someone was outside. But who? Who would be about at such an ungodly hour?

I swung my legs off the bed, pulled on my britches and boots, hitched up my braces, and set out to protect what was mine, if not to satisfy my curiosity. When I opened the door, I made out two men at the windmill trough. One sat on a crosspiece on the base of the tower, the other perched on the edge of the trough. I closed the door without a sound and walked across the yard. The one seated on the trough, I saw, was sipping from the cup.

"That is my water you are drinking."

The men started, stilled, then stood and took off their hats. One—I could not see well enough to know which—spoke. "We are sorry. We are weary travelers. Tired and thirsty. We mean no harm."

I stopped a short distance from them and strained to see more. One of the men was of a good size, both in height and girth. The other, slight. Each had a rucksack of sorts—the tall man's slung from his shoulder, the other lying at the smaller man's feet.

"There is a price to pay for drinking my water."

The men looked at one another. I could see now it was the

49

bigger man who spoke. "Your water? Surely water comes as a gift from God."

"Maybe so. But God left this water hidden under the ground. You are welcome to all of it you care to drink—but you will have to get it out of the ground yourselves, and not from my windmill."

They said nothing, only stood there, the big man shifting his weight from one foot to the other, rocking back and forth like a slow-moving pendulum on a clock about to run down. I let them stand for a moment.

"What are you doing out this time of day—hell, it is not even day yet—anyway?"

"We often travel at night, to avoid the worst of the heat."

I looked around and saw no wagon, no carriage, no horses, no mules—no means of conveyance whatsoever. "Travel? Travel how?"

"We walk."

"Walk? Through this desert? Are you addled?"

"No, sir. We are not. We are messengers for our Lord Jesus Christ."

That took a moment to consider.

"Where are you going?"

"Wherever the spirit sends us."

"And this spirit sent you here?"

The big man pursed his lips, considering a reply. "This way. We will pass through the mountain towns spreading the gospel message. Then on to California, where we will carry out our labors until called home."

I let that stew for a time. I confess I was somewhat baffled by the unusual situation. "Well. It is ten cents."

"Ten cents?"

"Each. For the water."

Again, the big man started in to swaying back and forth. "I

am sorry, sir. We have no money."

"What?"

"We follow the counsel of our Savior, as he taught in the tenth chapter of Luke. 'Carry neither a purse, nor scrip.' "

For the first time, the smaller man spoke. "The passage also forbids shoes. But we forego that counsel and pray not to be held to account for it."

I looked at the man. "So you can speak. I wondered."

He nodded. "I can. Mostly when called upon to testify of Christ. Or to voice a prayer. Other times, when the spirit so moves."

The growing light had revealed the big man to be of an age I guessed to be beyond thirty. The other, barely past being a boy. Their clothing was dusty and worn, the shoes even more so— the presence of their footwear looked to offer little more protection than its absence would.

I shook my head, whether in disbelief or disgust I could not say. "I guess you are welcome to the water. Drink all you need. And if you have canteens, you had best fill them. It is a far piece to the next water." I turned for the roadhouse but stopped when the big man spoke.

"Sir?"

I turned to look at him.

"Thank you, sir, for the water. The Lord will bless your kindness." He cleared his throat and shifted his weight some more. "We have been long without nourishment. Might the goodness of your heart include offering a meal to a weary traveler?"

My jaw may have dropped at the question. At least it was hanging open when I started working it in search of an answer. Finally, "Come on in. I will have the woman fix something."

The little man smiled. The big one looked even more sincere than before, if such were possible. "Thank you, sir. God will bless you doubly for your kindness."

51

I huffed. "I would much rather He pay the bill." I shook my head; again, whether from disbelief or disgust I could not say. "You can wash up there by the door. There is water and a basin. A towel to dry yourselves with. No soap."

The woman was up and about when I went in, working at the sideboard as though she already knew what was expected of her. The smell of coffee told me she had already boiled a pot. She stood at the sideboard with biscuit dough rolled out, cutting out rounds with a tin can.

I invited the men to sit, served them each a mug of coffee, then went out to the backhouse for my morning business. When I came back, the biscuits were in the oven and the woman was slicing bacon into the skillet. As it sizzled, she broke a dozen eggs into a bowl, looked at the big man, and cracked a half dozen more. She forked the bacon onto a platter and spooned some of the grease into a bowl for sop. Then she poured the beaten eggs into the skillet and stirred and turned them slowly as they cooked.

After filling my plate, I passed the food on the visitors. The big man went at it like a house afire, forking up eggs as fast as the fork would carry them, holding slices of bacon in the other hand, swiveling his head to tear off a hunk between every few mouthfuls of eggs. He ignored the biscuits until his plate was half empty, then forked open a biscuit, smeared half with bacon grease, and filled his mouth with it, gone in one bite. The other half of the biscuit got the same treatment. And again, with a second, then third, biscuit. Washing that down, and all that came before, with half a mug of coffee in one swallow, he turned his attention back to fork and plate. The other man could not match his companion in speed or quantity but matched him in intensity and enthusiasm.

With the table bereft of food, the visitors slid back from the table. The big man interlaced his fingers and perched his hands on his belly.

"As fine a meal as in my memory," he said.

The smaller man nodded and lifted his mug. "Is there more coffee?"

I filled all three mugs and sat back down. The woman had gone behind the curtain once the food was cooked. The big man looked that direction. "The woman—is she your wife?"

I shrugged. "More or less. Common law."

"She is a fine cook."

"Anyone can fry bacon and scramble eggs."

He nodded. "True enough, I suppose. But, hungry as we were, it is difficult to imagine a more pleasant repast." He sucked at his teeth as I watched him think. "Good food prepared by loving hands is surely a blessing."

I smiled. "Not sure there is much love in the woman. But she does her duty. Or pays the price. Are you gentlemen married?"

The small man shook his head. "Not as yet. But I hope to marry when we return home from our labors." He nodded toward his companion. "But he is blessed."

"How so?"

The big man squirmed in his seat. "I am married. Twice, as it happens."

"What happened to your first wife? Did she die?"

More squirming. "No. Not at all. She is well. Or was, when we left home. As was the other wife."

"Two wives. . . . Ah! You men are Mormons, then."

"As some call us. But, yes, we are of the Church of Jesus Christ of Latter-day Saints."

I shook my head. "Two wives. I cannot imagine it. Putting up with one woman is suffering enough for me."

"It can be a trial, at times." The big man smiled. "Listening to their incessant talk, talk, talk sometimes drives me to distraction. But your woman, she is a quiet one. Didn't say a word while you were gone, despite our questions."

I smiled and sat back in my chair. "She finds it difficult to talk to strangers."

"She is Indian?"

"Paiute. Sorry bunch of people if ever there was one. She would be living in a brush hut eating lizards were it not for me."

The little man's eyes darted back and forth as if my description troubled him. The big man pushed his plate aside, leaned into the table, and laid his forearms down, again lacing his fingers together. He gave me that sincere look and said, "Our church believes the Indians to be a chosen people—remnants of a band of wandering children of Israel. 'Lamanites,' they are called in our scripture. They are in the state we find them owing to the sins of their ancestors, turning away from the teachings of our Lord and falling into decay and disrepute. But there is a brighter day in store for them. They will rise up and take on the mantle of the Savior and become a white and delightsome people."

"Well, I would not waste any time waiting for such to happen to the woman."

The big man held up his coffee mug. "May I?"

I nodded, and this time he fetched the pot from the stove and filled our mugs.

"And what of you?" he said when he sat back down. "Have you religion in your life?"

I shook my head. "No. Not a speck of it. I was raised among Bible thumpers and had some teaching as a youngster, but it did not take. I see no profit in it."

"But surely you see the wisdom of Christ's golden rule—to do unto others as you would have them do unto you."

"I do not. My creed is to do unto others before they do it unto me. A man seldom comes out ahead if he does not watch out for himself."

"And the Ten Commandments given to Moses and the children of Israel by God himself? Surely a people guided by those laws will lead better lives than those who are ungoverned by any moral principles."

I stared into my coffee mug, looking for an answer in the dark liquid. "I could not recite the ten commandments. But I remember hearing about them. I suspect I have broken all ten of them at one time or another. Some more than others. And I will likely continue to do so."

The conversation continued, interspersed more and more with lapses of silence as the big man and I considered our answers. And our questions. The young man watched, wide-eyed and fascinated, as if such discussion had not been part of his teaching.

I offered this: "The teachings of God might be fine in books. But they do not hold up in the life of the world. All that nonsense about joy and happiness preachers carry on about is a rare thing, if there is any of it at all. The world I have witnessed is dog eat dog, kill or be killed, root hog or die. Why would a God make such a world? Or the people in it? Why would He promise love and happiness and joy and charity and all that other bullshit, and then not provide it? What kind of God is that, to deserve our acknowledgement, let alone our worship?"

After some deliberation, the big man said that the qualities I find missing in the world are absent owing to our failings, not God's. That He made the world and put us in it as a test of our character, not His. That He made us creatures of choice, with the freedom, nay, the necessity, to decide for ourselves how we will live—to choose good or evil, right or wrong, to love or to hate. That we owe Him homage for allowing us to prove ourselves. To ourselves, to our fellow man, to Him. That we fail is our sin, not His.

"Well," I said, "that being the case I have failed."

"You are not alone, brother. As the apostle Paul wrote to the Romans in the third chapter of his epistle, 'All have sinned, and come short of the glory of God.' "

"So we are all going to hell, then?"

"No. Oh no. There is hope for all. That is the good news of the gospel."

"I don't follow."

"Thanks to the grace of God and the atonement of Jesus Christ, we can repent. Our sins can be forgiven, and forgotten."

I suggested that might be true for your garden variety sin. But that I, as I told them, had laid waste to all ten of their Ten Commandments time and time again.

His look of sincerity more pronounced than ever, the big man said, "The prophet Isaiah told the world, 'though your sins be as scarlet, they shall be as white as snow; though they be red like crimson, they shall be as wool.' God truly can, and will, forgive and forget."

I brushed off the whole of it with a sweep of my hand. "Even if my sins can be forgiven, I cannot bury them deep enough to be forgotten." I rose from my chair and summoned the woman. I told her to put together a parcel of food for the men to take. From behind the store counter I dragged a big burlap bag across the floor and dumped it next to the table. Shoes tumbled out. Shoes for men and some for women. Boots and brogans and other kinds, sizes up and down the scale. Shoes I had accumulated, offering them for sale as need and opportunity arose.

"As you see, these have all been worn. Not a one of them is new. But they are all serviceable, to some degree. If you can find a pair to fit you, you are welcome to them."

The men smiled and pawed through the pile. Each found a fit, albeit the big man had to tug some to get into a pair of ankle-high lace-up boots. The young man slipped right into a pair of military-style boots, the heels scuffed from having carried spurs.

They walked away happy, freshly shod and provisioned for the road ahead. They passed the old well, and, as they did, the big man tossed the old, worn-out shoes he had walked in on down the hole.

Chapter Seven

No traffic came by on the road for days and days after the Mormons left. Then one afternoon as I sat on the step having coffee, I saw a haze of dust rising over the saddleback pass. Something was coming. I knew not what, for never before had I seen so much disturbance on the road.

I tossed the last of the coffee away and went inside. When I came out, I carried a shotgun loaded with double-aught buckshot in one hand, a Spencer carbine in the other, and a Colt Army revolver holstered at my waist. By then, a wagon and a half-dozen or so loose-herded horses had topped the pass and were coming down the long slope to the valley. After a few minutes, cattle reached the summit, strung out along the road, herded by a handful of cowboys.

The wagon stopped a quarter mile or so out on the plain. A cowboy spurred his horse into a lope to reach the horse band and turn them, bunching them up near the wagon, where the driver had stepped down to help hold them. The other mounted herders pushed the cattle off the road into the brush, circled them back on themselves, and let them stand. As soon as they stopped, some of the cows knelt down to rest. Others stretched their necks into the air and bawled. From the distance, I could see only that it was a mixed herd, cattle of all sizes.

I walked out into the road, out beyond the windmill, and stopped. One of the riders left the herd and came toward me at a trot. He reined up his horse some ten feet away and looked me over, then leaned out and set loose a stream of syrupy tobacco juice. He sat upright, pushed his hat up his forehead with a fingertip, then stacked his hands on the saddle horn.

He said, "This must be your place, mister."

I said yes and asked if the cattle were his.

"They are. Me and mine are comin' out from Arkansas. Them out yonder is my brother, my two oldest boys, and one of his. That's our uncle drivin' the wagon. Goin' to California to take up a ranch there. These cows be the seed stock for the outfit. Some beef steers to sell for cash. We'll be bringin' more cattle next year when we go back to fetch the womenfolk and young'uns."

His horse stood quiet, but alert and nervous, his ears erect and head high, nostrils flared. The rider leaned down and patted him on the neck, saying something quiet beyond my hearing. "You're mighty well armed for a man welcomin' company."

"It is lonesome out here. A man never knows what he might encounter. All kinds come on this road—not all of them come with good intentions."

"We mean you no harm." He nodded beyond me in the direction of the windmill. "Our only ask of you is to water our animals at yonder trough, and to refill the barrel on the chuck wagon."

"That many cattle will overrun my trough and break it down."

"We will hold the herd where it is and bring them in in small bunches. You needn't worry none. Them cows is used to bein' handled."

I considered what he said. Then, "There is the question of money."

The rider sat upright in the saddle. "Money?"

"Yes, sir. It is a thin living out here. Income from the water helps keep the place going. It does not amount to much, but it helps."

He mulled that over for a time, then leaned over and spat out another stream of tobacco juice. "And just what is it you ask for a drink of water?"

"Two bits a head for animals. Ten cents each for people."

His forehead furrowed, and the corners of his mouth arched downward, cutting creases that framed his chin. "Hellfire, mister! I got more'n two hundred head of thirsty cattle! You're askin' fifty dollars just to water 'em!"

"That. And it looks like another three or four dollars for the horses and men. I will overlook the filling of your barrel."

His laugh was without humor. "That's right kind of you." He spat again, the puddle of foul liquid staining the soil. "Thing is, mister, we ain't carryin' that kind of cash. I got a letter of credit from a bank back home, is all. A few dollars cash money, but it ain't nowheres near no fifty dollars."

I let him stew for a time. "You say you have steers among the cattle?"

"Some. We aim to sell them in California for cash to tide us over. Two- and three-year-olds, mostly. A few yearlings."

"Cut me out ten head of the older ones, and you're welcome to all the water you and your herd need."

He said nothing, but I could see the color creeping past the greasy rag around his neck and up his jaw and cheeks.

I said, "If you care to, I will even allow you to stay over and water the stock again in the morning—they will leave here rested and well watered. I suggest you do so. It is a far piece to water once you leave here."

"Ten head!" burst from his trembling lips. It was as if he heard nothing of what I had said since I spoke those two words. "Ten head! Mister, you know damn well that any two of them steers would bring more'n fifty dollars!"

I shook my head. "Not here. The truth is, I have no need for them. But cattle seem to be the only currency you possess, and there is the possibility I could find a market for them. Someday. Maybe. I could butcher one from time to time for meat, but there is little need for that."

For a good while he stared at me, eyes filled with hatred. He said nothing, but his jaws worked over the wad of tobacco. Finally, he spat again, then said, "How 'bout we do this—I kill you instead."

The Spencer rifle stood buttstock on the ground. The shotgun hung in the crook of my arm. I let the rifle lean against my thigh, moved a hand to the forestock of the shotgun, and lifted the barrel until the bores stared at him. I said, "How about we do this, instead. You hand me whatever it is in the way of firearms you are carrying, and I will not shoot you out of the saddle."

He raised his right hand, slowly reached back to the saddlebag, and fumbled around for the buckle without taking his eyes off me.

When finally he lifted the flap and reached into the mouth of the bag, I jostled the shotgun barrel. "Two fingers."

His hand came up pinching the grip of a revolver between thumb and forefinger. I walked over and took it from him and stepped back, releasing the cylinder and dumping the cartridges to the ground.

"Follow me." I walked slowly backward toward the windmill. He let his horse step often enough to match my pace. I leaned the rifle against the windmill frame and picked up a bucket and carried it to him. "What other weaponry do you have? The others, and in the wagon?"

"A pistol each. A Henry rifle in the wagon."

"That all?"

"That's all."

"Swear?" I said, jostling the shotgun barrel.

"Look mister, that's all the guns we got. I swear to it. On a damn Bible, if the likes of you has got one."

"You cannot blame me for asking. You did threaten to kill me." I stepped back and raised the shotgun. "Now, here is what you are to do. Take that bucket around to your hands and collect every sidearm there is. Bring them back here in that bucket. Loaded. Don't forget the rifle. And carry it with your finger well away from the trigger."

He spat, then turned and rode away.

"Mister!"

He stopped the horse, grabbed the cantle of the saddle, and turned to look back at me.

"You had best not try anything. There is a Sharps buffalo gun looking out the window of the roadhouse. And it is looking right at you."

I gathered the ejected cartridges from the ground and pocketed them, then walked to the windmill and engaged the gears to start it pumping. There was enough of a breeze to pump a good stream, so I did not worry about filling and refilling the trough as the cattle drank. Out on the plain, I witnessed histrionics and hollering among the cowboys as the man rode among them collecting their pistols. I could hear the sound of shouting but not the words, braided as they were with the bawling of the thirsty cattle.

The bucket dropped to the ground at my feet when the man returned. He handed me the rifle. I stepped back and jacked the shells out of the Henry rifle and put them into the bucket. I emptied the cartridges from the pistols into the bucket. As I worked, the rider sat in the saddle, watching. From time to time, he exhaled loudly, and his fingers drummed his thigh.

"Bring in your herd to water," I said. "And make sure not to overrun the trough. There will be water enough for all."

He spat. "We'll do as you say, by damn. The boys are cuttin' your pound of flesh from the herd now. Tell me where you want them penned."

I pointed out a corral in the yard behind the roadhouse. He told me they would bed down the cattle in the brush after watering them and water them again come morning. I pointed out a lone cedar tree standing by the road about a mile beyond the place and told him he would find his firearms there when they left. I wished him luck on his journey to California, and on his return to Arkansas for his remaining family and herds.

"I'll tell you this, mister. You can bet your ass that when we come back next year, we won't be takin' this road." He spat one more time for emphasis, then reined his horse around and spurred it into a lope toward the herd.

When the dreams awakened me in the dark before dawn, I slipped out of the roadhouse and walked out by starlight to the cedar tree by the road. With bits of twine, I hung the pistols and rifle from the branches like baubles on a Christmas tree, the ammunition hanging with them in a cloth bag. The cowboys were finishing up watering the herd when I went out back for the morning chores. I carried the Spencer carbine with me.

I kept watch for two days until I felt confident the drovers would not be coming back to seek revenge. The steers he left were quality cattle, well fleshed and carrying good weight in light of the many weeks on the trail and miles traveled. They plodded along docile when I saddled the old mare and drove them out to the canyon.

A few days later, the letter man came by eastbound. He sat at the table spooning up a thick stew the woman had stirred up the day before. He carried a thick slice of bread, setting it aside from time to time to sip from a bottle of beer.

He pushed back the plate after wiping up the last specks of gravy with what was left of the bread. "I'll have that coffee now," he said.

He locked eyes with the woman and gave her that half nod when she put the mug on the table. She gathered the soiled napkin and utensils, slipped them into the wash pan to soak, and crossed the room to disappear behind the curtain.

"What happened to her mouth?"

I stopped rearranging shelves behind the counter and looked his way. "Mouth?"

"Sure. That bottom lip looks to be swoll up. Cracked, too. You can tell it's been bleedin'."

With a shrug, I went back to shuffling store goods. After a bit, I dusted off my palms and put them on the counter. "Cannot say that I have noticed anything wrong." I smiled. "She has not complained."

The man shook his head and sipped his beer. He sat quiet for a time. Then, "Passed a herd of cattle on the way here. Man said they was bound for California."

I nodded.

"Said they come by here."

I nodded again.

"Said you skinned him near to the bone to water his stock."

I shrugged. "Same price as applies to all, had he paid cash. Fact is, he got a deal. Watered his herd twice. Filled his barrel for free. The man has nothing to complain about. He will not miss those ten spindly steers he culled from the herd."

He said no more. Sat nursing his beer for several minutes. Then he emptied the bottle, walked over to the counter, and pretended to inspect the goods on the shelves. "I see you still got that soap there."

I did not respond.

"Wouldn't hurt to unwrap one of them cakes and put it out with the wash basin."

I turned and looked at the soap, then at the man. "Wouldn't

hurt you to scrub a mite harder with plain water. This is not a bathhouse."

He pulled a leather purse from his pocket and fingered out coins to cover food and water. He held them in his palm, pushed them around with his finger to count and count them again, then let them rain down on the counter. They rang and rattled and bounced and rolled across the surface. One coin rolled off the edge and fell to the floor. He watched it wobble across the floor and stop, lodged in a crack between floorboards. The man fetched it and slapped it onto the counter.

"You know, mister," he said, "one of these days you will fleece the wrong man. You may well end up dead."

I shrugged. "I compel no one to trade here. If they do not like my prices, they are welcome to move on."

"You know damn well that can't happen. Leastways so far as water is concerned."

"If not for me, that windmill would be nothing but a broken-down wreck. I am the only reason there is water here at all. Like I said, they can pay me for the privilege or they can go thirsty."

He stared at me longer than was comfortable. I followed him to the door and leaned against the frame, watching him tighten his saddle girth, untrack his horse, and mount up.

"You'll recall that I already paid to water my horse."

I did not reply.

He gave me that half nod, turned, and rode to the trough. He did not dismount as the horse dipped its muzzle into the water to drink.

Chapter Eight

When my eyes opened, I found myself sitting upright in the bed. I knew not what had awakened me. Or why I trembled. Perspired. Panted. I knew only that it was nothing of the present world that disturbed my sleep. Rather, a dream. One of those dreams whose effects linger even as all memory of it is lost.

The woman crawled from the bed, lit a candle, and followed its glow across the floor and through the curtain. She returned in a moment, a glass of whiskey in hand. She knelt on the bed, lifted my hand in one of hers, wrapped it around the glass, and held it with me, raising it to my lips. Her dark eyes sparkled candle flame. She pressed the glass into my hand and loosened her grip, reached to the bedside table for a rag, and sponged the sweat from my face and forehead, and wiped the sting from my eyes. She lay down on her side, curled with arms cradling knees, and watched me from her pillow.

I sat in the puddle of bedcovers sipping the whiskey. When the tremors stopped and my breathing became regular, the woman rolled over and snuffed out the candle. In no time at all she slept, breaths rattling in her throat.

But I—I would sleep no more.

Any traffic on the road was an event. But to see a two-horse surrey wheeling along the rutted trail inspired wonder. The buggy all but glowed with color. Red and green and yellow—

hues nowhere a natural part of this place.

It drew closer. The driver was a woman. A woman of ample size, shaded under a hat of even larger proportions, redder than blood, trimmed in red of deeper shade, and banded with fabric flowers of white. Gloved to the elbows in white, the sheaths showed smudges and stains of hard wear. Her dress was as red as her hat and likewise trimmed in red.

In the rear seat were two younger women, one dressed in green, the other yellow—those shades as saturated and brilliant as the driver's red. They, too, wore hats, though not so substantial in size as the driver's. Long tendrils of red hair fell from beneath one hat to hang over a bare shoulder and tickle the edge of the revealing neckline of a green dress. Besides the fringed top of the surrey, an unfurled parasol shaded the girl. The woman in the yellow dress had pinned-up hair as black as the gloves she wore. She leaned against the other and looked to be asleep.

A platform hung from the back of the surrey, stacked with trunks, cartons, cases, carpetbags, and hatboxes. The mismatched team of horses in harness looked serviceable, but nothing more. Lean, but not bony, they were worn down and in need of rest. The horses did not need much encouragement to stop when the driver tugged on the lines.

The driver looked around the place and settled her gaze on the windmill. "That good water in that trough there?"

"As good as it gets."

"These plugs could use a drink."

"Two bits apiece. A dime from each of you ladies, if you care for a drink of water."

She did not react. Said, "How 'bout a bait of grain for the horses? You got that?"

I nodded.

"Food for me and the girls?"

Another nod.

"How 'bout a place to sleep?"

I shook my head. "This is not a hotel. We have no sleeping arrangements. Most folks who stop by are happy to pitch a tent or roll out a bedroll in the yard."

She nodded. "Well, I reckon we can sort something out." She shifted her backside on the seat and turned to the women in the back. "Girls, water the team and unhitch the buggy yonder by the building." She turned back to me. "Where'bouts you want we should put these horses so's they can get that grain?"

I pointed out a pen beside the barn and said where they would find the grain bin inside. She told the young women to tend to it, then meet her inside the roadhouse.

"There's water and a washbasin and a towel there by the door, if you would care to freshen up. No soap. You can see the backhouse out there, if you need it." I smiled. "I guess I should say 'when' you need it, you being women and all." If they saw any humor in what I said, it was not evident.

"Thank you, sir," the driver said. "It will be a pleasure to sit for a change. Squatting in the sagebrush ain't all that ladylike."

The woman was already stirring up a batch of cornbread when I went inside. A pot of beans and ham bone simmered on the stove. I fished sour pickles out of the crock and filled a dish, then skived the rind of mold off a chunk of cheese and cut some slices. Such would be the bill of fare for supper.

I sent the woman away when she finished the cornbread. The women came in together and looked around the room as they made their way slowly to the table. When they sat, I carried the steaming pot of beans around the table by the bail, ladling out a plateful for each.

"There is coffee to drink," I said. "Water. Whiskey, corn and rye. Rum. Bottled beer, but it is not cold."

They all opted for coffee, and I filled the mugs. The two

younger women had yet to speak a word in my hearing, but, once they opened their mouths to eat, the talk came tumbling out as quick as the food went in. Their humor was coarse, their language unrefined. Snide comments on the likely effect of the beans on their digestion—the likes of which you might hear from cowhands in a cow camp—amused them for a considerable period.

Still, the company was more pleasant than that which usually populated the place, and I enjoyed watching and listening. I imagined whiling away an hour or two in counting the freckles on the redheaded girl's bare shoulders and back—and wherever else they might appear. The natural-born charms of the young woman in yellow were no less enticing.

The driver called for rum all around when they finished eating. I fetched a bottle and glasses from the counter.

"You ladies mind if I join you in a drink?"

The younger ones looked at one another and giggled. "I don't think all of us can fit into one of them little ol' glasses," the one in yellow said, setting off another round of hilarity.

"Please. Join us," the driver said. "Pay no attention to these two. Seems like they forgot whatever manners I taught them."

I poured drinks for the ladies, then fetched a glass for myself and pulled up a chair beside the driver and opposite the others. I filled my glass and raised a toast to our collective good health, and we exchanged salutations for several rounds.

"How came you ladies to be on the road?"

The driver swirled her glass and watched the rum spin. "Had me a saloon. These girls worked for me. Mines mostly petered out years ago. But I been hangin' on by the skin of my teeth. Thinkin', like some of them miners, that the next round of dynamite would open up a new vein." She swallowed the last of her drink and signaled me to refill the glass.

I topped off the drinks all around.

She said, "Never happened. Leastways not enough to change anything. For the better, that is." Another taste of the liquor. "The less ore there is, the less need there is for whores. So I sold my place for less than the wood to build it cost."

"Where are you going?"

She shrugged. Took another drink. "Don't know for sure. Colorado, maybe. Black Hills. Who knows? Hell, we just might keep goin' till we get to Saint Louis." Now, she giggled like the girls. "Or Boston, even."

We drank some more. And some more. By now it was evening outside and nearly dark as night inside. The driver said they had had enough hospitality for one day and asked me to total up what they owed. I walked with more care than usual to the counter and lit a lantern. I fetched the stub of a pencil and tore a sheet from the back of an old ledger book I had acquired somewhere. I stumbled once on the way back to the table but managed to stay upright. I set the lantern on the table, rolled the pencil lead around on my tongue, and attempted to list the charges.

The task was more than I could muster up the concentration to complete. I finally gave up and dropped the pencil. I wagged my head, staring at the paper.

"We will settle up in the morning, if you do not mind."

The driver smiled. "I've got a proposition for you."

I rousted the woman out of the bed and told her to find somewhere else to sleep. Where she bedded down, or where the driver found to sleep, I do not know. Nor did I much care at the time.

It was crowded with the three of us in the bed. I did not care much about that either. I will only say that both of those young ladies were accomplished at serving up horizontal refreshments. I finally fell asleep trying to count that redhead's freckles by candlelight.

When the surrey wheeled away in the morning, I watched it stir up dust all the way across the flat and up the long slope to the saddleback pass.

The women would not run short of water on the road, as I had lashed a keg of it alongside their luggage and supplies and whatnot on the back of the buggy. And tied a canvas sheet over the lot to keep out the dust.

The quartermaster sergeant from the fort showed up later that same day. When I saw him riding in with his patrol on the narrow trace from the north, I told myself to take care not to let my good spirits get in the way of negotiating a profitable deal on whatever he was looking to acquire.

I said nothing when the mounted soldiers lined up along the trough to water their horses. Experience had taught me that, when dealing with the army, it is best to just add it to the bill as some miscellaneous charge. If they quibbled, I knew I could make it up next time. But you can bet I always kept track in my head.

The troopers sat in the shade of the barn smoking and playing mumblety-peg while the sergeant and I conducted business.

"That all you need? Ten head of horses?" I said. "That is hardly worth my time to drive them to the fort."

"Don't need no more at present. Plenty of remounts available elsewhere if you don't care to fill the contract."

"You will pay more to get them elsewhere. You know my prices are always in your favor."

"I know it. That's why I rode clear the hell down here." He stood from his chair and swallowed the last of his coffee. "But if you don't want to sell . . ." The sergeant shrugged and set his mug on the table and started for the door. I let him get halfway across the room, thinking he might relent. It did not look likely.

"Sit down. I am sure we can come to some sort of agreement." I refilled his mug, taking my time as I thought. "What about beef?"

He blew the hot off his coffee and took a sip, his brow furrowed. "We got plenty of beef to feed us at the fort." He took another sip. "I could use some cattle for the Indians—they got an allotment comin' up."

"How many head do you need?"

"Twenty ought to do it."

"I believe I can come up with twenty head of prime beef. For a price."

The sergeant laughed. "Hell, it don't need to be no prime stock. These is Indians we're talkin' about feedin' here. Any cow critter on four legs'll do, so long as it's able to stand on those legs long enough for them Paiutes to slit its throat."

"All the same, I can supply twenty head of good steers, two and three years old. Maybe one or two yearlings, but no more."

"That, and the ten head of remounts?"

I nodded. The sergeant walked to the stove and refilled his mug.

"I could sweeten that up for you."

He hesitated and stared into the mug, as if there were any question on the matter. We haggled over terms. The sergeant agreed to a bit of a premium for the horses—still well below what he would have to pay elsewhere. As usual with our arrangements, I was to bill the army at a price closer to the market value of the horses. The quartermaster sergeant would pocket the difference. The way he saw it, I made a profit and the army got a good deal, so there was no reason why he should not make a little money from the arrangement, as well.

I could not fault that kind of logic.

Negotiations for the cattle were more complicated. I was not accustomed to selling beef to the army—but I had those ten steers from the drover and no other way to dispose of them.

Filling the rest of the order would deplete my own herd somewhat, but I would replenish it over time.

Market prices for cattle were firmer than for horses. And the government set limits on what it would pay to provide for Indians, despite what the treaties promised. And the army had regular contracts with suppliers of beef, which would complicate things for the sergeant. None of that mattered a whit to me, so long as I came out ahead on the deal.

We agreed on delivery dates and exchanged a handshake, and I signed some government forms for the sergeant to fill in later. Government paperwork was of no interest to me. Let him earn his money dealing with the bureaucracy. Like I said, I did not care about the details so long as I made a profit. The last thing the man did before leaving was refill his pocket flask from my whiskey bottle.

The quartermaster sergeant led his patrol back up the trail toward the fort. I watched the dust rise from the churning hooves of the trotting horses, glowing golden in the low angle of the evening sun as it slowly sifted back to earth.

Footsteps coming and going and going and coming. The squeak of hinges and clatter of a door latch. Muted laughter. Angry voices. Slaps. Cries. Moans. The creak of bedsprings. The boy rolled in the bed for the last time that night. Trousers hiked up and shoes in hand, he stepped through the back door and into the yard. Thought better of walking farther. He sat on the step and pulled tight knotted laces on battered brogans. Across the fence, light from windows and pole lamps waxed and waned through wisps of river fog.

He walked to the alley gate, crushing shards of glass underfoot. Broken bottles, bereft of beer, whiskey, laudanum, tossed unwanted out windows.

When the boy returned, the backyard twinkled like star shine as glints of sunlight played off broken glass. He looked through the kitchen window, his own reflection superimposed over the face of his mother. She sat opposite at the table, glassy eyes staring at something beyond the pane, somewhere remote from the world.

He plucked empty flagons and jars and flasks from the table and dropped them into the rubbish bin by the door. Pulling out a chair, he sat, elbows propped on a tabletop now empty save two bottles of tincture of opium and their stoppers. One bottle lay on its side, a droplet hanging from the lip. The other stood, as empty as the other.

His mother had not moved. Stared, still, out the window. He looked into her eyes and saw no life there. She tipped when he touched her shoulder, sagging to the table and stopping only when her head struck unrestrained. He watched her for a moment, and, in a moment, she crumpled in the chair, tipped, and fell inanimate to the floor.

CHAPTER NINE

After she cleaned up following breakfast the next morning, I told the woman to saddle up the old mare.

"Get your ass over to the reservation and that sorry excuse of a village where your kin lives. Tell those useless brothers of yours I have some work for them." I told her if she couldn't find her brothers—which I knew, of course, that she couldn't—to get a couple of cousins or uncles or whoever the hell else she could find who could sit a horse and follow a cow and not get lost on the way to the fort. "Then you get back here. If you are not home by tomorrow night, I will come for you—and you will not like it if I do."

The woman had no more than faded into the distance when a rider leading a pack animal topped the saddleback pass. I watched as he came down the long slope and across the flat, and I walked out past the windmill to meet him. He rode a McClellan saddle cinched to an old brown horse, the lead from the sorrel pack mule tied to a ring behind the cantle. The mule carried a bulky load, its nature concealed beneath a rumpled sheet of oiled canvas secured with an off-kilter diamond hitch. Both the animals and the rider looked trail weary, heads hanging low as they plodded along. The horse stopped unbidden, and the rider looked up.

"Mornin'," he said.

"And a good morning to you, sir. How can I be of assistance?"

He looked around the place, scratching at a scruff of hair on his face, either an undecided beard, or the result of several days' laziness in employing a razor. "We'll just set a spell. Take a rest 'fore movin' on."

"Early start this morning?"

He nodded and dismounted, then untied the mule's lead rope. "Mind if I give these critters a drink at your trough there?"

"I do not mind a bit. But it will cost you twenty-five cents each for the animals. Ten cents for yourself if you care to drink."

The man did not react—at least not in any noticeable way. He just held me in a heavy-lidded stare for the longest time. He finally led the horse and mule to the trough and watched as they buried their muzzles in the water. I handed him the cup, and he held it under the pipe to fill.

"You know, mister, I don't recall whenever I paid for a drink of water."

"Well, you are welcome to find a drink elsewhere if you find the price objectionable."

He emptied the cup in a couple of long swallows and handed it to me. "What I am thirsting for is coffee. My supply run out two days ago. My damn head's been poundin' ever since. I wonder if you've got any of that elixir."

"I do. There is a pot on the stove as we speak, fresh this morning. And I can sell you beans or ground coffee to replenish your stores, either one."

"Your prices as steep for coffee as for water?"

"Well, sir, since coffee is mostly water, I charge the same— ten cents. The flavor boiled into it comes gratis."

The horse and mule stood, water dripping back into the trough from their muzzles. He said, "Pour me a cup."

We walked to the building, and he looped bridle rein and lead rope over the hitch rail. I nodded toward the washbasin and pitcher on the shelf by the door. "There are water and a towel there if you care to wash up. No soap."

The coffee was already poured when he came inside. Like most visitors, he stopped to look around the room before taking a seat at the table. He cradled both hands around the mug as if absorbing its warmth on a cold morning. He lifted the mug to his nose and inhaled deeply. Only then did he sip from the mug. He set it back on the table, hands still wrapped around it. He closed his eyes and sighed.

"Damn. I needed that."

"I can sweeten that up for you, if you like."

"You mean sugar?"

He sipped again, taking in more this time.

"That. Or molasses. Honey. Whiskey. Rum."

The man smiled, almost laughed. "What? And foul this here perfectly good coffee? No. In fact, not just no, but *hell no.*"

"As you wish," I said with a shrug.

For a man as deprived of coffee as he led me to believe, he took his sweet time about drinking that first mug. Not that I minded. I was curious about the man and hoped he would linger, at least for a time.

I said, "What is it that brings you to this country?"

"Survey. Only preliminary, though. If my reports is favorable, they'll send out a regular survey crew to fill in the details."

A survey. The notion intrigued me. Rather than reveal my curiosity, I got up and went for the pot and refilled his mug. "What kind of survey? The road has been in use for years. Railroads abandoned any interest in this part of the country a long time ago."

He sipped his coffee. "I am not at liberty to say much. Kind of hush-hush, if you know what I mean."

I said nothing. After a minute or two, he talked again.

"I don't guess it will hurt anything to say there's an outfit lookin' for town sites."

Without meaning to, and unable to stop it, I scoffed and snorted at the revelation. "Town sites? Who the hell would want to live in this country?"

"Well, there's you," he said with a half smile.

I nodded. "And, for that fact, I can tell you that it is no easy life. And I have a reliable source of water, which cannot be said of many other places in this desert."

"Well, now, that's the thing. This outfit, they got a notion they can claim whatever springs and runoff streams they is and impound the water in rezavoys. Engineer canals and ditches. Lay out towns, and farm fields."

After mulling it over for a time, I said, "I do not see how that could work out here."

"Worked for all them Mormons in Utah Territory. Hell, they got towns strung out all along them mountain ranges over there."

"But the Mormons have a lot of manpower to do the work. Work they don't have to pay out for, given their way of doing things—working for the common good, like they do. Most people will not do so. Most people would rather take care of themselves, and never mind the neighbors."

He shrugged. "That is as it may be. And I ain't sayin' you ain't right. But that ain't my lookout. I got my job of work to do, and what happens after that will happen. Or it won't."

I pushed my mug away, long since having had my fill of coffee. "The load that mule is carrying—surveying equipment, then?"

He nodded. "Some. Scopes and compasses and such for location. Barometer for elevation. Maps. Just enough for me to lay out for the outfit what's out here, so's they can see what possibilities there is." He waved a hand as if brushing the subject away. "How 'bout you warm up this here coffee I'm a-drinkin'. Then tell me again what you got in the way of coffee that ain't been boiled as yet."

I filled his cup, wondering in my mind how many times I had done so since he sat down. I shook the pot, and there was little left in it to slosh. I asked him to step over to the stores, and he followed me, setting down his mug on the counter and his hands palms down on either side of it. I hefted a forty-pound bag of java beans from under the counter to the top.

"Good beans, these," I said. "I can sell you as many as you need."

"I don't know. I ain't never got the knack for roastin' beans. I believe I gets too eager and scorches 'em in the skillet. Coffee always tastes burnt. 'Sides, I ain't got a grinder."

"Do not concern yourself about that. I have a grinder right here." I turned toward the shelves to fetch it, but he stopped me.

"Never mind—unless you ain't got none of the stuff ready made."

"Sure thing." I slid the bag of beans off the counter and held back its fall to the floor. I produced two one-pound paper bags of roasted and ground coffee. "Take your choice. There is Arbuckle's, and there is Folger's. You could not go wrong with either variety."

"Folger's, eh? Ain't never heard of that."

"It comes from out in California. Some prefer it. Me, I find both varieties acceptable. I believe what you have been drinking is Folger's."

The man mulled it over. "How is it you have so much coffee away out here?"

I shrugged. "This, that, and the other. Buy it from freighters that still come through from time to time. Trade travelers for it when they find themselves needing something more than they need the coffee."

He laughed. "I can't see how that could be. What might a

body need more than coffee?" He hitched up his pants and placed his hands back on the counter. "Give me a couple bags of that Folger's stuff."

"Certainly. I can give you a better price on the Arbuckle's, if price is a concern."

"All right, then. All the same to me. Two bags of Arbuckle's."

I put the Folger's back on the shelf and fetched another bag of the other. "Will there be anything else you are needing? I can supply most any want."

He nodded. "I can see that. This'll do."

I suggested we settle up and proceeded to itemize his purchases aloud.

He reached to his side, to retrieve a purse I suspected. Rather, his hand came up clutching a pistol, and he pointed the business end of it at me.

"I got a better idee," he said. "How 'bout I pay you your price for the coffee I drunk and these here bags I'm takin'. But I am damned if I will shell out a penny for the watering of my stock. That just ain't right, chargin' folks for water."

"You intend to steal from me?"

He ratcheted back the hammer. "I sure as hell do, if that's what you want to call it. I'd as soon steal from you, as you steal from me for a drink of water."

I grabbed his mug of coffee from the counter and tossed the burning liquid into his face. He reared back and pulled the trigger, the bullet plowing into the ceiling. He was swiping at his face, trying to wipe the coffee from his eyes when I came up from behind the counter, shotgun in hand, and discharged both barrels into his chest. The blast knocked him from his feet and carried him a fair distance before he hit the floor, and he kept sliding across the planks when he lit.

He wheezed a few breaths, and his feet and legs quivered a time or two, but there was no life left in him. I broke open the shotgun, thumbed out the spent shells, and set them on the counter, the hulls still wisping powder smoke. From under the counter, I fetched an open box of shells, refilled the barrels, and stowed the gun and shells back underneath the counter.

I dragged the surveyor out the door and let him lay. Back inside, I studied the blood puddle on the floor. I fetched the water bucket from the shelf by the stove and sloshed it into the blood. With the woman's stiff broom, I scratched at the wet mess, then threw down some old rags to sponge it up before any more of it could soak into the floorboards. It took another bucket of water and some time on hands and knees scrubbing, but I got up the most of it. If it still showed any red when dry, I would spill some oil or something on it to change the stain. I threw the rags into the bucket. When they dried, they would burn in the stove fire.

Turning my attention to the surveyor, I rifled his pockets and came up with a bit of cash and a serviceable clasp knife, but there was nothing else save a few pebbles and stones of curious appearance. I pulled off his boots to keep, but his pants were so stained and snagged and patched as to be worthless. His shirt, of course, was obliterated, at least in the front. The back, I assumed, would be as bad or worse. His hat, which didn't show much wear, was a Dakota-style Stetson with a "Montana Peak" crease in the crown. It fit me snug. I looked inside the crown and pulled out strips of paper he'd stuffed into the sweatband. I tried it on again, and it settled into a perfect fit. A man can always use a good hat.

After untying the hitch on the pack mule, I laid out the canvas sheet, grabbed the surveyor under the arms, dragged him onto it, then rolled up the corpse and cloth and hefted him onto the horse. It did not help that the smell of blood upset the horse, and he danced around snorting and tossing his head. But, finally, I lifted and pushed the man until he lay belly down across the horse's back. I led the horse to the old well, it shying and sidestepping the whole way. Stopping beside the rock rim wall around the well, I stepped to the side of the horse and shoved off the load. The horse sidestepped, and the surveyor landed atop the rock wall and rolled off into the dirt. I larruped the spooked horse across the face with the bridle reins and kept up the lashing as he skittered backward away from me, hind quarters down, head up and thrashing back and forth, ears pinned back, wall-eyed, and nostrils flaring. I stopped the flailing and jerked the bridle reins until the horse stopped, then led the quivering beast over to a pen near the barn and wrapped the reins around a fence rail, adding a half hitch for good measure.

Back at the well, the dead surveyor lay face down. I grabbed the canvas with both hands and lifted him up and laid him over the rim, then lifted the one end and pushed until his weight over-balanced, and he slipped and slid into the darkness below.

CHAPTER TEN

The McClellan saddle went astraddle a pine pole rail in the barn with other saddles and tack I had accumulated. I checked it over carefully for any identifying marks but found none. It looked to be army surplus, of which there were plenty about. Its presence should not arouse undue suspicion, even though a stock saddle suitable for working cattle was the usual riding gear in this country.

Most of the camp equipment and food supplies in his packs went into my stores. I sat for a time tinkering with the surveying machinery. The compasses and some of the scopes made sense to me, but there were instruments whose function I could not fathom. Some had his name etched into the brass or other metal fittings, and those went down the well. I loaded the rest of the lot into an old packing box and hauled it out back and into a shed full of a variety of such junk I had no use for, but which might hold some value to someone, someday. You never know who might come along.

When I came out of the shed it was coming on evening, and the man who carried letters was watering his horse at the windmill. I waited for him at the door of the roadhouse. He led his horse over and stopped.

"Got anything to eat in there?"

"The woman ain't here." He looked disappointed. I said, "I believe I can rustle up something. I have yet to eat, myself."

He nodded and asked if I cared where he penned his horse.

"I just traded for a dun horse and a mule. They are in the corral attached to the barn. I do not know as yet how they will act around other animals. It may be best if you put up your horse somewhere else. He will be all right in with those horses and cattle in the big corral, if you do not mind his being in with them. Or, one of the empty pens farther back if you would rather. Farther to carry feed and water, but it is up to you."

The man did not answer, other than that half nod of his. He led his horse out back. I went inside and dipped some hardboiled eggs out of the brine jar, dished up some pickles, sliced some cheese, carved some ham from a joint the woman had been working on, and found a package of crackers on the store shelves. I heard the man washing up outside as I tossed another handful of grounds into the coffee pot and filled it with water. He came in as I shoved in some stove wood, fanned up the flames, and clanged the door shut.

When I looked up, he was standing at the store counter fingering the spent shotgun shells I had left lying there. He lifted one to his nose and sniffed it.

"Doin' some shootin' I see," he said, putting the hull back on the counter.

I nodded and wiped my hands on the towel the woman kept hanging on the oven door. "Varmints. We had a fox trying to get into the chickens. We trapped that one, but I believe there may be another one showing up. Maybe a coyote. I heard a ruckus out there last night and took a shot in the dark. Both barrels."

"Hit anything?"

I told him no and invited him to sit and eat.

He stacked a piece of cheese on a cracker and took a bite. "Seen a lot of hoof prints and footprints and drag marks out by the old well," he said as he chewed. "What you been up to?"

I hoped he could not see the twinge I felt. I stood and went to the stove, licked a finger, and tapped the side of the coffeepot. "I believe this is ready," I said and filled a mug for each of us. "Just disposing of some old junk out of a shed. Muck from the corrals."

"This here's a regular kind of bachelor meal, for certain," he said as he bit into a pickled egg. He swallowed. "Where's your woman?"

"Oh, she has gone to the reservation to visit her kin there."

Again, with the half nod.

"When's she comin' back?"

I pushed back from the table, started to rise, then sat back down. "You sure ask a lot of questions for a man whose business none of it is."

He shrugged and laid a slice of ham on a cracker, took a bite, and chewed it slowly. He took a drink of coffee. "Just makin' conversation is all. Don't mean nothin' by it."

We finished the meal, such as it was, in silence. He pushed back his chair and stood. Coins from his pocket purse jingled to the table, and he counted off what he owed.

"I'll likely be gone 'fore sunup," he said, then walked to the door and opened it. Before stepping out, he turned back. "I'll be rollin' out my bed out back. Don't you be unloadin' any more of that buckshot thataway in the night."

I do not know why I woke up when I did. It might have been the sound of hoofbeats as the man rode away in the dark that disturbed me. Or it may have been a dream. I raked my fingers through hair damp with sweat, lay down flat on my back, and listened to the receding sound of falling hooves and the drumming of my heart.

No one came by that next day. Including the woman. I fiddled around the place, watching the road. I had no appetite for food, so I drank a few bottles of beer. Later, I sat at the table and uncorked a bottle of whiskey. I must have dozed off, for when I woke up, there I sat. The old mare whinnied, and I realized the woman was back, and her coming must have disturbed my sleep.

I lit a lantern and went out to the barn. From the look of the stars, we were well into the night and coming on morning. The mare was tied to the hitch rail, unsaddled, and the barn door was ajar. I went in, and the woman had just thrown the saddle over the rail and was fumbling around for a gunnysack to rub down the horse.

She did not jump when I hollered, so she must have heard me coming. "Where the hell you been? I told you to be back yesterday."

Her eyes glinted in the lantern light when she turned to look at me. But the gleam in her eyes looked more like internal fire. She turned away, and I hung the lantern on a peg and picked up a pitchfork. I prodded her backside with the prongs to get her attention, then reversed my grip and laid the handle upside her head. The woman stumbled but did not fall, so I swung again. The handle bounced off her shoulder. She sat down, arms wrapped around her head. I landed repeated blows on her back and arms until the effort wore me out. I stabbed the pitchfork into the ground.

"Finish up with the horse, then get the hell inside," I said between hard-drawn breaths.

She came in with the old rawhide parfleche she always carried slung over her shoulder. She dropped it next to the wood box and built a fire in the stove and readied the coffeepot and put it on the heat. Trimming the wick and lighting a lantern, she next picked up her egg basket and went out the door. It was still pitch dark when she came back in and put a mug of coffee in front of me. She unwrapped a slab of bacon and sliced some into the skillet and pushed it aside when nearly cooked and cracked four eggs to fry beside it. From somewhere unbeknownst to me she produced a loaf of bread and cut off two thick slices, which she dropped into the skillet after lifting out the eggs and bacon. The whole of the food she cooked slid in front of me on a plate, and the woman topped off my coffee and sat down opposite me.

Despite the aftereffects of the whiskey I'd drunk yesterday and last night, the food went down easy. I pushed the plate away after every trace of the meal, right down to the last smear of egg yolk, was cleaned off it. The woman got up and poured me some more coffee and sat back down.

"You find somebody to come drive that stock for the army?"

She nodded once and held up two fingers.

"Your brothers?"

She shook her head "no" and shrugged as if she knew not where they were.

"These people—are they coming today, like I said?"

She nodded and proceeded to flap her hands around. I never did get much of the knack for sign language, but I thought she was telling me something about her mother or a cousin or some such. I waved her away and told her I did not care if it was the man in the moon who came, just so he could do the job.

By now the sun was lighting things up, even though it was yet to rise. I told the woman I was going to ready the stock for the drive. When her Indian friends came, she was to send them on north up the trail toward the fort. I gave her some landmarks— which she already knew about—to watch for, and if I was not already there with the herd, they were to wait for me there.

Figuring the old mare was spent from the woman's trip to the reservation, I saddled another horse I knew to be gentle. I haltered the dun horse I got from the surveyor. His mule, I figured, would follow along without a lead. They would stay out in the canyon until I found a buyer or some other use for them. By the time I was ready to ride out, the woman had a sack of food and canteen of water ready.

The steers I gathered out of the herd in the canyon came easily enough, even though they seemed reluctant to leave the easy grass and water there. Cutting out ten head of horses proved a bigger challenge, unwilling as they were to abandon the other horses. Still, I had the horses and cattle out of the canyon and loose herded on the sagebrush flat when the Indian drovers arrived. One was the woman's uncle—the one I had thrown off the place and told not to return. Given the need for drovers, I decided not to object to his presence. The other was a boy, a young man, I suppose, who looked to be of an age to be the old man's grandson, or perhaps son.

"Do you speak English?"

The boy nodded. "I do. Father understands the white man talk and speaks it well, as you know. But he chooses to no longer speak to you."

I asked him how the woman had come to recruit them for the job, rather than her brothers—knowing full well the brothers were no longer available for this, or any other, job.

He said no one had seen the brothers for some time and did not know of their whereabouts. "No one of the people in our village wanted to do this work for you. But your woman and my father are family—he is her mother's brother. I believe you know that. She convinced him to do this work, even though he did not want to."

Through all the conversation, the old man stared at me, and if his eyes blinked even once it escaped my notice. Then he turned and looked at the boy, and nodded.

The signal must have meant something, as the boy said, "How much will you pay for this work?"

I named the wage I had paid the woman's brothers to drive stock to the fort. The man said something more in Paiute to the boy. The boy looked at me and looked back to his father. The father talked to him again. The boy looked back at me, back at his father, who furrowed his brow and nodded, then back at me, although he would not look at me directly.

"My father says it is not enough."

"The hell! It is the same as I paid them blanket-ass brothers of hers. They never complained."

The man said something to boy. The boy said, "My father says you cheated the boys if what you say is true. He says we will go home if you will not pay more."

"How much more?"

Again, the man talked to the boy, and the boy talked to me. They wanted the same amount as I offered, but for each of them. We talked back and forth, me claiming I would go broke paying that much, them claiming they would go home with empty pockets rather than work for what I offered. We finally settled on a price half again as much as my original offer.

I would have sent them away empty handed had I not felt the need to be at the roadhouse should someone happen by on the road. I gave the boy the paperwork—bills of sale and receipts and such—for the quartermaster sergeant and sent them on their way. Both looked at ease horseback and experienced handling stock as I watched them push the cattle and horses into a bunch and start them up the trail. I turned my mount in the opposite direction and headed back home.

It was dusk when I got there, but light enough that I saw from a fair distance someone at the windmill. I reined up and took a brass telescope from my saddlebag and extended the draw tubes to take a look. Parked by the stock pens was a Murphy wagon. It looked to be the same one that had come through before, the outfit I had sold an ox to replace the lame one. I shifted the view to the windmill, and there stood the freighter, leaning against the tower while two yoke of oxen stood side by side with their heads in the trough.

I slid the telescope shut and spurred the horse into an easy lope as I floundered around getting the spyglass back into the saddlebag. When I rode into the yard, the freighter had lifted the yokes and turned the four oxen into an empty corral.

"Good evening," I said.

"And you," the freighter said as he latched the corral gate. "I reckon you know these critters has had their heads in your water trough."

I nodded.

"Not surprised," he said. "You probably got that water all measured out by the drop so's you can tell if there's a thimbleful missing."

"Well, not quite that precise. But I calculate your oxen there drank about a dollar's worth. I would not care to speculate as to whether there is a dime's worth missing from the trough and in your belly."

"Truth is, mister, if you was to check that tin cup you'd find the bottom of it damp yet. I confess to wetting my whistle. I talked to the woman in the place, there, when I rolled in, but she never said yes or no. Never said a word, far as that goes."

"I was led to believe when you left here before that you would not be stopping by again. Which you did not on your return trip."

He walked behind his wagon and dropped the tailgate. "Well, here's the thing. Figured I may had just as well save the water in my barrels, since I wanted to stop and check on that ox of mine I left here, anyway. The one with the bad hoof—I'm sure you ain't forgot him."

"No, sir. How is that ox I sold you doing?"

"I got to admit he's a good'n. Pulls his share of the load and maybe a little more. He's an easy keeper, too."

I smiled. "I am glad to hear it. A satisfied customer is always a thing to be desired."

"I said he was a good ox," he said as he slid a kitchen box

out of the wagon and set it on the ground. He looked up at me. "I never said I was a satisfied customer." He swung the tailgate shut and latched it. "I aim to camp here tonight if you've no objection."

I said it would be all right, and he asked if I minded him building a fire.

"Just so you don't burn the whole place down," I said. I told him there was a ring of rocks in the yard where many a traveler had kindled a fire. He asked about firewood.

"There are split logs and kindling under the woodshed there," I said, pointing out the roofed-over woodpile, as if he was not already aware of it. "There is a cost for that. If you do not care to pay the price, you will find a pile of scrap lumber out beyond where the wagons are parked. You are welcome to break up and burn all of that you need. No charge."

He nodded. "What about that ox of mine?"

"He is better but still lame. I do not know if he will ever heal up altogether."

The freighter lowered his head and hitched his thumbs in the bib of his overalls. "You think he ain't fit to travel as yet, then?"

I shrugged. "I would not think so. You can take a look at him in the morning and see what you think."

"I daresn't even think what the feed bill'll cost me to get him out of here."

I turned the horse toward the barn. "We can talk it over come the morning. We will settle up for the water then, too. Firewood, if you burn any." I tapped my heels against the horse's sides, and he shuffled toward the barn.

The freighter stood, thumbs still stuck in his bib overalls, watching us go.

CHAPTER ELEVEN

The sun was not yet showing its face when I walked out into the yard, coffee steaming in the mug I carried. The freighter was burying the dead fire in the pit. I knew he had already watered his teams, as I'd watched him do so from the roadhouse. He scraped loose dirt over the ashes and tamped it down with the back of the shovel blade. He stood and faced me and stood the shovel beside him, holding the handle in one hand and stabbing the point into the ground.

"Mornin'," he said.

I nodded and sipped my coffee. "Looks like you are ready to go."

The ox teams were yoked and hitched to the wagon. He slid the shovel into its leather slings, tacked to a sideboard on the wagon.

"Looks like." He handed me a dollar and a dime. "I never burnt none of your wood."

I pocketed the money.

"I had a look at that ox. I believe you're right that he ain't fit to travel." He took off his fancy hat and slicked and mopped the top of his bald head with a wadded handkerchief that went back into the pocket of his overalls. "I reckon I'll look him over when I come back from the mines." He hesitated for a time. "How bad you goin' to screw me over for his keep?"

"Will you be making another haul this way, after this one?"

He shrugged. "Couldn't say. Depends if them miners over

the way think they'll scratch out another load of ore. Might take 'em a while to do it. Might not do it at all."

"Well, we will talk on your way back. See if you have any better idea." I took another drink of coffee. "The thing is, we do not see much out here in the way of fresh food, save meat. And eggs, when the hens lay. The woman's garden does not ever yield much. Some years, not at all. If you make another trip, and could see your way clear, bring us a sack or two of potatoes and a bag of onions, and maybe some carrots. Do that, and we will call it even."

The freighter looked pleased at the prospect. Said if he came out this way on another run, he would surely do just that. Said orders from the mining towns were so slim he had plenty of room in the wagon. We shook hands, and he said he would stop on the way home and let me know the outlook for another ore-hauling trip.

He released the brake lever and put the ox teams into motion with a click of his tongue, a command to "get up," and a wave of the goad. As the wagon rolled out of the yard and onto the road, the sun climbed above the mountains, shining hard light on the tail of the wagon and casting shadows for the freighter to follow across the valley.

The Paiute drovers made it back from delivering the cattle and horses. The money bag from the quartermaster sergeant held the agreed-upon payment in gold and other coins. I settled up with the Indians, and no sooner was the money off the table than the woman slid plates of stew made from dried deer meat and desiccated vegetables in front of the three of us. She set out a plate of biscuits and refilled our coffee mugs.

The old man babbled something to the boy, and the boy said his father wanted to buy some cartridges. He put an 1860 Army Colt on the table. The old cap-and-ball pistol had been converted to take cartridges. The cylinder was scratched up. Much of the bluing on the barrel had rubbed off, and the walnut grips were missing, replaced by a rawhide strip wound around and around the handle.

I harrumphed when I saw the state of the pistol. "You sure you want to risk firing that thing? Looks to me like it is as likely to blow up in your face as fire."

The man only stared at me with dark eyes that revealed nothing. But the firm set of his mouth said there would be no discussion of the matter. I fetched a box of .38 caliber cartridges from the store shelves. He pushed a gold coin I had paid him with across the table, and I made change for him.

I told the boy I would likely have more work for them in the future. Both he and the old man nodded approval. The woman handed them a sack full of biscuits and cold bacon left over from breakfast, and they rode away.

The woman dished herself up a plate of stew and sat down at the table to eat. She watched as I fetched the cash box from under the store counter, got the key down from atop the lintel over the window, and stowed coins from the army business in the box, and put it all back again. What the woman did not know was that most of the gold coins, and others I had accumulated over time, never saw the inside of the cash box. Rather, the bulk of my gains were tucked beneath the false bottom of an old steamer trunk under a pile of blankets and clothing in the corner of the bedroom.

A week or so later I saddled the old mare and rode out to the box canyon to check the stock there. I wanted to assure myself that the cattle and horses had settled back into the routine of eating and drinking and sleeping after the upset of cutting out and driving off some of their number. All looked to be well as I rode through the animals.

As I neared the spring and old cabin, a yearling buck deer raised his head from drinking. I reined up and sat still, hoping the muley would believe the mare was just another one of the horses wandering the canyon. When the deer again lowered its head to drink, I swung a leg over the cantle and, as I stepped down, slid my rifle from its scabbard. Using the saddle seat as a rest, I waited for the young buck to raise its head again, then fired. The bullet hit low, just behind the shoulder, and must have plowed right into the heart, for the deer folded its legs and went down where it stood.

I thought to hoist the deer from a limb on the cottonwood tree and gut it. But I decided the offal would draw scavengers and did not care for the possibility of attracting coyotes or bobcats or even a mountain lion into the canyon where they might harass the herds. So I slung the carcass whole over the saddle bow and rode out of the canyon. When well away from the mouth, I hung the deer from a cedar branch and let out the entrails and clotting blood, cut off the head and lower legs and leave them lay, then loaded the lighter weight of the carcass back over the forks of the saddle and rode for home. The woman would be busy for a time, butchering the young deer and smoking and drying the most of the meat.

It must have been about a fortnight, maybe three weeks later, when the bank robber came. No one else had been by on the road, save the letter carrier, who stopped only for water, and the freighter on his way home. He allowed as how there would be at least one more trip for ore and would see about supplying the root vegetables we talked about when he came this way again.

I was forking manure out of the small corral attached to the barn when a man came riding in from the east. His horse was all but staggering, the rider prodding the animal with his spurs and lashing the rump from side to side to side with the tail ends of the bridle reins. He did not stop at the windmill. Instead, he pushed the horse on to where he saw me working.

He dismounted the stumbling horse and was pulling loose the latigo almost before he hit the ground. "I need me a horse, mister."

"I can see that. Looks like you have been needing one for some time."

"Cut the bullshit. I see you got horses. I want one."

"I am happy to oblige. But it will cost you. How much are you willing to spend? The better horses will cost more, of course."

"Like I said, cut the bullshit." He pulled a pistol and pointed it my way, drawing back the hammer for emphasis. "I want the horse with the most bottom. He'll be in for some hard ridin'. And that's your pay, standin' right there," he said, gesturing toward the spent horse with his pistol barrel.

I laughed, but the return of the pistol my way cut it off.

"Grab your saddle, and step into the barn. There is a horse stabled there that will suit you."

"You first. Get a move on."

Keeping the pitchfork in hand, I stepped through the gate and walked into the dim barn. "Why all the hurry?"

He picked up the saddle by the gullet with his free hand and followed. "Not that it's any of your damn business, but I guess it don't matter none." He dropped the saddle. "Robbed a bank. Damn U.S. marshal been on my tail since. Sonofabitch won't leave off no matter what. I stole that useless sumbitch of a horse at a ranch I passed, but he never gained me any time, even bein' fresh. Been better off with the horse I had."

I unlatched the gate to the stall and led out a leggy bay horse that I intended to put back in the pen when I finished cleaning it. The robber holstered his pistol and looked him over, going so far as to lift every leg and examine the hooves.

"These shoes need to be reset."

"I am no farrier. But they do not look that bad to me. Besides, you are in no position to be choosy."

When he stood and faced me, likely with some other smart remark tingling his tongue, I forced all four tines of the pitchfork through his rib cage. His eyes widened, and he looked surprised. He looked down at the streaming blood, then back up at me. He blinked once, then twice. He opened his mouth to say something, but, rather than words, blood poured out of his mouth, tracing its way through his whiskers to drip off his chin and jaws.

Figuring the lawman he mentioned would be along before too much longer, I lowered the robber to the floor, stepped on his chest, and pulled out the pitchfork. Not knowing how much time I had, I decided not to take the body out to the well. I dragged him by the legs into a dark corner of the barn and tossed his saddle atop him. Then I covered him with an old wagon fly and rumpled it up so it looked to be tossed there, rather than concealing anything.

I practically had to drag the horse he rode in on into the barn and into the stall. The bay horse went back into the corral outside. I fetched a little water from the windmill trough in a bucket and set it inside the stall for the horse—just enough to take the edge off his thirst, but not enough to do him damage, overheated as he was.

Then I went to the roadhouse and poured myself a cup of coffee and sat down on the front step to await the arrival of the law. I was still sipping from the same mug, and the coffee was still hot, when I watched him ride over the pass, down the long slant, and onto the flats at a long trot. I walked out to meet him at the windmill. He said nothing, just stepped down from his horse and picked up the cup, dipped it full, then invited his horse to drink from the trough.

"You know, mister, that that water you and horse are helping yourselves to belongs to me."

He shook a few drops from the tin cup and hung it back on the nail. He tipped his hat back and looked around before speaking. "This here your place, then?"

I nodded. "Part and parcel. Including the windmill and the water it pumps."

He nodded. "I see." He peeled back his vest to reveal the badge pinned to his shirt. "As you see, I am a United States marshal."

"So?"

"I am here on official business."

"That makes no difference to me. I am here on business, too. And you owe me thirty-five cents for the water. A quarter for the horse. A dime for you."

"Well, here's the thing, mister. Like I said, I am here on official business. And I don't give two shits about you or your water. You ain't gettin' one red cent from me. And if that don't suit you, you can contact the law. You can file your complaint with me, and I'll see that it makes its way through the system. Then someone else up the line can tell you to go to hell, since it don't seem you'll accept that response from me." He stared into my eyes until satisfied I understood. "I'll be fillin' my canteen, too, if you'd care to add that to your complaint."

The marshal let his horse drink again, then led it away from the trough. He rubbed up and down the horse's legs and checked its hooves. He rocked the saddle side to side and snugged up the cinch, then mounted. He looked down at me and asked if anyone had been by here today.

"There was a rider came through a while ago. Looked to be in a big hurry. Barely stopped long enough to water his horse. He refused to pay, as well."

He asked what the man looked like, and I gave him a good enough description he would recognize the robber, but not good enough to imply I had seen him more than briefly. "Who was he?"

The marshal tugged the front of the brim on his hat, pulling it down over his forehead. "He's a bank robber. Robbed a bank a few days back. I been on his tail ever since. Damn near caught him a time or two, but he slipped away."

"Must have made off with a pile of money," I said.

He shrugged. "Enough to make it worth runnin' him to ground."

"Is there a reward?"

"Bank put up five hundred dollars."

I swallowed hard. "Dead or alive?"

"Why? You know something you ain't tellin' me?"

"No. Just curious."

"Well, truth is, the reward ain't for the man—it's for the money. Payable upon return of what he stole."

He watched me to see how that affected me. I did my best to remain passive.

"Guess I'll be gettin' on. I aim to catch that thievin' bastard before he gets someplace where he can spend that money. Should be soon—he ain't all that well mounted."

He turned the horse onto the road and turned back in the saddle as he rode away to say, "I'll be sure to file that complaint for you. About the water."

The marshal smiled and tipped his hat and rode off down the road after his prey.

CHAPTER TWELVE

The marshal rode away, and I watched him go until he turned from a dot in the distance into a memory. I was not convinced he was gone for good. If he was any kind of a tracker, he might soon notice the absence of all sign of his quarry. But, believing the robber was nearly within his grasp and saddled with a jaded horse, he may well ride headlong into failure and frustration before realizing the bandit had somehow faded into emptiness.

Giving either prospect equal weight, I did not return to the barn that day in case of being watched. Nor did I visit in the night, nor throughout the next day, save to haul a bucket of water to the horse penned there.

The following night, however, found me making my way to the barn in the dark of night. Once inside and behind a closed door, I lit a lantern and lifted the canvas covering the bank robber and his saddle. I dragged the man by the ankles into the open area. His boots and spurs were all in good repair—neither the footwear nor the gut hooks showed much use. Off they came. His shirt and trousers were likewise recent purchases. The pockets contained nothing of interest or value. After laundering by the woman, the trousers would go on the shelf. Four bloody holes across the bib of the shirt rendered it useless.

I doused the lantern and waited for my eyes to adjust to the dark, then opened the door and stepped out into the night. Neither hearing nor seeing anything out of the ordinary, I went back inside. I took the bandit by the arm and slung it around my neck and lifted him up until the body slumped over my shoulder. Pausing again outside the door until convinced it was safe, I carried him to the old well and dropped him over the side. I listened as he scraped down the sides of the shaft until the distant, hollow thud of him bottoming out echoed up the hole.

Back inside the barn, I lit the lamp again and untied the saddle strings and pulled the saddlebags loose, then set them aside. Their heft felt promising. I studied the saddle for any identifying marks. Cut into the stirrup fender, concealed by the skirt, was a name. Whether the name of the robber or not, I knew not and did not care. A saddle whose past could be traced was of no interest to me, so it, too, went down the well. I did save off the oxbow stirrups and the cinch.

Inside the roadhouse, the saddlebags hit the floor behind the counter with a satisfying thunk. It was all I could do to let them lie until morning. I tucked in beside the woman without disturbing her snores and soon fell asleep. I do not know how long I slept, but there was little rest in it. I awoke in the gray light with heart pounding, shivering as if cold, even while clammy with sweat. I gathered up shirt and britches and boots, pushed aside the curtain and walked to the table, where I sat on a chair and dressed. A few sticks of kindling and some blowing on the coals got the fire in the stove going, and I fed it a few chunks of wood. The coffeepot soon boiled, and I fed it a handful of fresh grounds to mix with the old and set it aside to ripen.

If anything could alleviate the abstract uneasiness I felt after the fitful sleep, it would be the contents of the bank robber's saddlebags. I fetched them from under the counter, and, again, the clunk as they hit the table sounded hopeful. I fumbled with the buckle and laid back the flap. Bundles of paper money tumbled out. In the bottom of the bag was a sack of gold and silver coins. The other pocket held much the same, as well as a bag with an odd assortment of paper bills and loose coins.

I poured a mug full of coffee and sipped it as I stared at the bounty. I separated the money into stacks and piles. The amounts in the bundles of paper money were printed on the bands. The coins divided into even stacks covering most of the tabletop. All in all, it represented a payday surpassing many times over the five-hundred-dollar reward the marshal said the bank offered for its recovery.

Back into the saddlebags it all went. When the woman staggered out from behind the curtain to fix breakfast, I carried it all to the bedroom, pulled the pile of blankets off the top of the old steamer trunk, emptied it out, and pulled up the false bottom. The money filled the hidden chamber beyond its limit, so some of it went back in the saddlebags to await a new hiding place. It was a problem for which I did not mind seeking a solution.

The marshal came back two days later. I was not concerned. All trace of the robber was gone, except his horse. And it was just another nondescript brown horse among a few other nondescript mounts in the big corral. I met the marshal at the trough at the windmill and asked if he had got his man.

"No. Sumbitch just disappeared off the face of the earth. Nobody saw him on the reservation—leastways no one claimed to. Hadn't noticed if any horses got stole, neither. There ain't enough people left in them mining towns that he could've gone through there 'thout bein' seen." He shrugged. "Damned if I know where he got to."

"Well, that is unfortunate. I would not mind getting my hands on that reward you talked about. Five hundred dollars is a lot of money."

He agreed. "I don't suppose he come back through here after I left."

"No. As a matter of fact, there hasn't been a soul come

through on the road since you."

He looked around the place, looking over the barn and outbuildings. "Mind if I have a look around here?"

"Of course not. Although I cannot imagine why."

"Plenty of places to hide out."

I laughed. "I would have seen him—or the woman would have—if he had been hiding here."

The marshal stared at me for an uncomfortable time. "It may be that he ain't hidin' from you."

"What? Are you saying I have been concealing him?" I felt the flush climb my face. "Go ahead! Look around all you want. Then get the hell out of here."

He mounted his horse and started toward the barn and outbuildings.

"One more thing," I said.

He stopped and turned his horse and looked back.

"You owe me another thirty-five cents for the water. Dime for you, quarter for your horse."

The mail carrier came by the next day. I saw him coming down the slope from the pass and watched him plod across the flat, then walked out to meet him as he watered his horse. He greeted me with his half nod and said, "How come is it I don't never bring any letters to this place?"

It seemed an unusual question to me. But, like they say, if the only tool you have is a hammer, everything looks like a nail. I decided it was just that the mail occupied an outsized place in his mind. "Oh, there is not anyone trying to reach me. Nor is there anyone I need to correspond with."

"You ain't got no family nowhere?"

I said no, and he asked about the woman.

"She cannot write. Cannot read, either. And the only people she knows are on the reservation. She rides out there from time to time to visit."

He mulled that over. "Well, keep in mind that if ever you want to send a letter, I'll carry it to the post office for you. For all that, I can carry a message to the telegraph office when I'm goin' that way."

"Yes. And I suppose you will charge a pretty penny for the service."

He smiled. "Just the goin' rate. Which is a hell of a lot less than what it costs to get a drink of water hereabouts." He looked to the sky, checking the position of the sun. "What you got to eat in there? I just might have me an early supper before goin' on. Or, guess you could say it's a late dinner. Either way, I could eat if your woman is cookin'."

The man mounted his horse and rode along beside me as I walked to the roadhouse. I saw no need to remind him of the location of the washstand. He would likely just complain about the absence of soap. Inside, the woman dished him up a plate of beans seasoned with bacon, and a rasher of fried bacon to go with it. For bread, on offer was a choice of stale cornbread or bread sliced from a loaf. He took both. A bottle of warm beer washed it all down.

"Say," the man said between spoonfuls of beans, "I passed a U.S. marshal on the road. Said he'd been by here."

I saw no need to respond.

After another bite, he said, "Lookin' for a bank robber. Said he gave him the slip somewheres on the trail." He ate some more. "Said he thought he might of been hidin' out here."

"He implied as much. Even went so far as to search the place. He found nothing, of course."

He gave me a half nod and went back to eating. After cleaning up two helpings of beans, he asked for coffee. He settled up for the meal and water and stopped at the door. "I know that marshal some. He ain't the kind to give up easy. And he's suspicious of you, now. Was I you, I'd watch my p's and q's. That lawman is likely to come back here."

"Well, he will not find anything."

I stepped outside and watched as the mail carrier mounted up and rode away. He never looked back. But he did veer off the road to circle around the old well, stopping long enough to lean out of the saddle and look into the dark hole. But the depths swallowed all light and there was nothing to see.

The man carrying the mail, on his return trip, was the only traffic on the road for at least a week. Then one day, as I was carrying water to the stock in the big corral, a wagon came rattling in from the direction of the mining towns. It was a curious conveyance, a tall, square-sided box with a roof, like an oversized delivery wagon such as they use in the cities. It was painted up with flourishes and curlicues like a wagon from a medicine show, but without words, and the colors were faded and worn with more paint missing than there. Drawn by a lumbering mule between the shafts, the wagon rocked from side to side, and the wheels squealed for want of axle grease. A man in a battered stovepipe hat sat on the seat, wrapped in a linen duster. Long hair dangled under the hat, but the man was clean shaven.

The driver pulled the lines taut and stopped the wagon at the windmill. He removed his hat and cradled it in one arm. The top of his head was as bare of hair as the sides and back were fertile with it. He cleared his throat. "Sir, I have traveled a long and lonesome road, and the motive power of my mule is flagging owing to want of water. I, myself, am thirsty as well. May we imbibe from your wellspring of refreshment?"

"That is a lot of fancy talk to ask for a drink of water."

He dipped his head toward me and said, "My apologies, sir. Loquaciousness is a character trait I have refined to a fault, I fear." He replaced his hat. "But the fact remains, the mule and I are desirous of a drink."

"Help yourselves. Ten cents for you, a quarter for the mule."

He wrapped the lines loosely around the brake handle and stepped down. Doffing his hat again, he said, "My intention is to abide for a day or two, perhaps three, to rejuvenate the mule and reinvigorate myself. May we settle our accounts at my departure?"

I looked the man over, studied his wagon, and noted the condition of his mule. "Are you sure you are good for it?"

"I assure you, my good man, you will be amply satisfied with the recompense received. For the water, as well as any comestibles we may dispatch, and provisions we purchase to press on in our travels. Upon my honor."

After some thought, I invited him to use the water and pointed out where to park the wagon beside the roadhouse. I met him there with a grease bucket I had salvaged from one of the wagons in the yard.

"Your wagon needs grease. You may as well take the bucket. Then you can avoid that infernal squeak. Besides, the box and skein on your wheels and axles will last longer. So will the wheels and axles themselves."

"Thank you, kind sir. I am aware of the importance of lubrication. Unfortunately, a lubricant container, much like this one, that once dangled beneath the wagon was either purloined by some nefarious character or, perhaps, plucked from its proper place by some object, unseen or unnoticed, in the road while traveling. In any event, thank you, and please include the grease bucket among our purchases."

I told him to turn the mule into the big corral, then to come on inside after he tended to the wagon. "You will see a washstand by the door. There is water and a towel there. There is no soap."

"No soap. Oh, dear. My hands will likely be soiled after

lubricating the wagon. I am not sure water alone will clean them."

"Well, I can sell you some soap if you need it."

"Ah, yes. Please do set a cake of the cleanser by. Add it to my account, of course." He turned toward the wagon, rolled up his sleeves, and hitched up his trousers. "I shall see you inside, post haste."

CHAPTER THIRTEEN

The woman had a hen stewing. It was a rare thing. The times she served chicken bordered on never, so the hen in the pot must have been old and long past her egg-laying days. I told her to get a meal together, as we had a paying mouth to feed. She stirred up some fat and flour and by the time our visitor finished with his wagon and had washed up, a plate of chicken and dumplings awaited him at the table.

"A most toothsome repast," he said. "Ambrosia to the soul, as well as the palate. You are to be complimented most effusively, madam."

The woman gave him a curious look, then turned back to her business of cleaning up.

"I detect unfamiliar seasonings, my lady. A dash of some secret spice that adds relish to your medley of flavors. Might I inquire as to its identity?"

This time, the woman did not even look. Sliding his plate away and patting his tummy with both hands, the man said, "Ah, the confidential knowledge of the chef. I fully understand your reticence to reveal your culinary mysteries."

I could not help but scoff. "It's not that. She does not talk."

"You mean she is not fluent in the elocution of the English language? I discern her origins are among the indigenous people of our nation."

"Paiute. But that is not it. I mean she does not talk at all. Her tongue was cut out."

His sudden intake of breath seemed to inflate his eyeballs as they widened under arched brows. He recovered from his surprise and said, "What precipitated such a savage circumstance?"

I shrugged. "Punishment. I suppose she said too much some time—or said the wrong things to the wrong people. Maybe sassed someone once too often. There is no understanding Indian ways."

Swallowing the last of his coffee, still looking pale, he asked about other "libations."

"If it's a drink you want, I have whiskey, rye or corn. Rum. Bottled beer—but it isn't cold."

He asked for a "dram of corn liquor," and I poured him a glass. He tossed it off in a gulp, and I poured another. He finished that one off just the same and asked if I had any wine. I told him we were out and had been for some time. It had been a long spell since any of it had come to hand. I poured him another glass of whiskey.

"That wagon of yours," I said. "It is an odd-looking affair."

"Refurbished and converted according to my precise directives, corresponding to the necessities of my profession."

"And what might that be?"

He sat up a little straighter in his chair. "I capture light reflected by objects within the frame and preserve a permanent facsimile of their image."

My blank expression prompted a simplified explanation.

"In the most elementary of terms, I am a photographer."

"I see. What do you take pictures of?"

"I do not *take pictures*. I make photographs."

I asked the difference. He launched a lengthy and mostly indiscernible explanation, peppered with fancy words like shapes, textures, patterns, contrast, curves, lines, symmetry and asymmetry, depth of field, foreground and background, viewpoint, negative space, perspective, and other such pompous prattle.

Then he said, "That truncated, and somewhat simplistic, explanation pertains only to the artistic sensibilities and aesthetic principles involved in the making of photographs. There is required, as well—and equally important in the process—conversance with the sciences concerned. Primarily, a comprehension of chemical composition and the properties of interactions when elemental constituents are blended—"

I held up my hands to stem the onslaught. "Please," I said. "All these big words are making my head hurt. Let us call it good for the day. Maybe tomorrow you can try explaining it again."

He smiled. "Better than an explanation, kind sir, I shall offer a *demonstration*."

"I cannot wait," I said. Which, of course, was a lie. But he was a paying customer, and given the size of his account already, and the probability that it would grow larger, I would steel myself and listen to what he had to say come the morning.

Morning was a long time coming. I do not remember how many times I awakened short of breath and filled with anxiety. The sky was yet gray when the photographer stepped through the door. Under his arm was what looked to be a stack of boards, thin and painted black. He set them on the table as I poured him a mug of coffee.

After a few sips of coffee and some comments on the morning that used up a lot more of the mother tongue than necessary, he slid one of the boards from the pile—two of the boards, I should say. They were, as I had thought, thin sheets of painted wood. But they were hinged together in pairs with leather and lined with felt or flannel or some other soft fabric. Each enclosed several photographs.

He lifted the pictures one at a time, grasping them by the

edges with his fingertips, and set them on the table, telling a story about each one—where and what it depicted, when it was "made," and other such. I confess the photographs were beautiful, and I was soon engaged in the display and in the accompanying explanations—despite his usual spewing of so many words, many of which were unfamiliar to me.

There were photographs of mountains. Rocky slopes riven with canyons, rugged peaks covered with snow, thick stands of trees, grassy meadows rimmed with pines, mirror-like lakes reflecting their surroundings so clearly it was difficult to tell which end of the picture was the top and which the bottom. He had photographs of buildings. Log cabins in the woods, fancy houses in town with filigree and latticework, commercial blocks on city streets, even entire towns and cities as seen from some high point. There were sweeping desert landscapes: row after row of mountain ranges fading into the distance, wide alkali playas, seas of sagebrush surrounding mountain islands, gnarled cedar trees silhouetted against white skies, even blooming buds and flowers, some atop spiny cactus plants.

And people. Not the typical, staged studio portraits one usually saw. His photographs showed people posed more or less where he found them. There was a picture of a bartender standing alone behind his polished bar framed by a mirror and rows of sparkling bottles and glasses lined up on a showy back bar. A preacher clutching a Bible outside the door of a church with a looming spire and cross. A sheepherder perched on the steps of his camp wagon with a herding dog curled up at his feet. Cowboys squatting and spraddled around a campfire in a roundup camp. There was a photograph of a half dozen miners standing next to the headframe over a mine shaft. I recognized three of the men—the Chileno I took for a Mexican, and his two partners who once stopped here. He showed me a picture of a trio of tarted-up girls seated around a table in an empty saloon. An Indian family, with a child atop a bony horse and a man standing by holding the bridle reins, and a woman next to him holding a baby wrapped in a blanket.

While we looked through the collection of photographs, the woman stirred up a batch of mush and fried some bacon for our breakfast, and boiled fresh coffee. The photographer stacked his photographs out of the way of our bowls when she served us. On top of the pile was the picture of the Indians. She saw it there and all but spilled my mush. She stood upright and gasped, her hands covering her mouth. The photographer looked at her with wonder.

"What is it, woman?" I said.

She pointed at the picture and tried to talk, the noise babbling about in her mouth like an excited hen stuck under a bucket.

I slapped the table. "Dammit, woman! Hush up!"

She drew a sharp breath and started in to waggling her hands and fingers as if trying to shake off hot water. I could only make sense of about half the signs, if that.

"She is saying something about those Indians in that picture, there," I told the confounded photographer. "Something about their being her kin, but she has not seen them for a long time."

The photographer picked up the photograph and held it out toward the woman, but she shied away from it. "Holding it will not inflict any harm, I assure you, dear lady. The photograph merely captures the likeness, the image, of these personages. It does not, despite the conjecture of some of your people, steal the spirits of those depicted."

So he told her, but, still, she would not take the picture in hand. She was content to view it from a distance, and then only with sidelong glances, as if the people in the photograph might resent her staring directly at them.

With the pictures tucked safely back into their protective

wooden folds, the photographer invited me to visit his wagon for an explanation of its functions in the making of photographs. I do not know if it was excitement at having a somewhat interested audience, or that he had a store of language locked up he was eager to turn loose, but he was insistent.

He first set up a tripod and mounted his camera. It looked much like others I had seen—little more than a wooden box with a bellows with a circle of brass-framed glass attached to one side and a drape of black cloth hanging from the other. Alternating between fiddling with the front end of the camera and ducking under the drape, he satisfied himself with whatever he was doing. Then he lifted the drape and invited me to take a look.

The back side of the camera was a sheet of glass, not clear, but dull, as if coated with something. I saw nothing on the glass until lowering the drape. I threw off the fabric. "I see the windmill!" I said. The photographer only smiled. I ducked back under and looked some more. After a time, I came out from under the cover. "It is the windmill, all right. But it is upside down. And backward—the trough is on the wrong side."

"That is so. It is the same with all cameras."

"But why? Why does the camera not see what I see with my eyes?"

He cleared his throat, took a deep breath, and his eyes sparkled with a smile his mouth barely registered. "It is a matter of physics. The essence of photography is the seizure of light rays reflected by the objects within the frame. To reach the plate that records the image, those rays must pass through the aperture of the lens, which is centered on the optical axis. Since the propagation of light is rectilinear, the rays continue on their straight paths unchanged by the aperture. Thus, light rays from above reach the aperture on a downward path, those from below on an upward path, and so on, left, right, and center. The rays illuminate the glass—and, when a photograph is captured, the plate—at the conclusion of their journey, opposite their orientation at origination. Up appears down, left appears on the right, etcetera and so on."

I could only stare at him.

"One grows accustomed to seeing the world so, and the juxtaposition becomes virtually unnoticeable. I, in fact, am of the opinion that it aids composition—the unfamiliarity of the scene allows one to analyze balance and arrangement and other qualities based solely on aesthetic considerations."

I continued to stare, as yet to even blink.

"Well, then, enough of this and that. Please, do me the honor of stepping inside," he said as he gestured toward his wagon.

We stepped inside, and he shut the door. The place was as dark as death.

He was accustomed to the cramped quarters and knew his way around in the dark. The scratch of a lucifer match cast some light, and he touched the flame to a candle, which brightened things up a little more, but just enough to make out that the walls were lined with shelves, and a counter ran along one side. The photographer opened a nearly flat box he took from a shelf and unfolded a little wire frame covered with red cloth. It opened into a tall, thin box that looked to be built to stand over the candle. He slipped it over and into the base that held the candle, then put a lid on top and covered the hole in the lid with a little metal plug-like thing that kept the light in but let the heat and smoke out. The gadget killed most of the candlelight, leaving only a dull, red glow lacking the strength to even cast a shadow.

"Much of making photographs involves laboring in near darkness," he said. "As I have previously stated, photography consists primarily of the capture of light. Therefore, the absence of light is required in the process, for should the light-sensitive materials be exposed to unwanted illumination, the desired image will disappear, overwhelmed in an overabundance of luminosity. The dim, red light provides some visibility, but is too weak to endanger the photographic materials."

"Whatever you say."

"Would you be amenable to a demonstration of the making of a photograph?"

"I suppose so."

He reached up and raised a lid on the ceiling, and the flood of sunlight through the square hole was enough to cause me to squint.

"The first step does not require darkness."

He opened a cabinet and pulled from a slotted box holding several of the same a sheet of glass and held it up to the light and looked it over. "This is, as you see, but a piece of glass—a fused substance of mutually dissolved silica and silicates. Nothing more than a windowpane, really. However, by employing the collodion wet plate process, it will become a photosensitive plate and provide the means to record the scene we have seen through the lens of the camera. Were it not simple science, it would be the stuff of magic, mystical, even." He expounded on the fragility of glass, and how its cracking or breaking, whether in its initial state or after becoming a photographic negative, was one of the hazards of the traveling photographer.

Next, he uncorked a bottle of orange syrupy-looking liquid and dumped a puddle onto the middle of the piece of glass, which he tilted back and forth to spread it all over the glass, talking the whole time in words that mostly escaped me. I do recall he said the whole business from then on had to be done in about a quarter of an hour, before the "plate" dried. He then reached up and dropped the lid on the ceiling. I could not see much of what he was doing, but he said he was bathing the coated glass in silver nitrate or something or other. The air in the wagon turned foul. After a couple of minutes, he clamped the glass in a frame, which I would soon see, once my eyes adjusted to the light outside, fit onto the back of the camera. He slid a tin sheet out of the frame and stepped to the front of the camera and took a little cap off the lens. After a few seconds, he put the lid back on, stepped behind the camera, and slid the tin sheet back into the frame, took the frame off the camera, and hustled me back into the wagon.

I stood just inside the door with my arms tight against my sides, as there was little room, what with his scurrying back and forth along the counter pouring stuff out of bottles into little trays. He took the glass plate out of the frame and slid it into one of the trays and rocked it back and forth, washing the liquid over the glass.

"Look!" he said after a few seconds. "There appears your windmill!"

I looked, and it did not look like much. The glass was mostly black, with gray smudges and a few white lines that looked like they might be the mill tower. The photographer lifted the plate out of the liquid he called developer, and into another tray of plain water to wash it, then into a third tray of "fixer" so it would stay the way it was. Of course, he used a whole lot more words to explain it, but you get the gist of it.

"Unlatch the portal, and we shall scrutinize the result of our efforts."

I opened the door, which is what I figured he had asked me to do. At the same time, he opened the hatch on the ceiling. He squeezed into the inadequate space beside me and held the plate up into the bright light.

"Ah, yes!" he said. "From all appearances, we have achieved success."

"It doesn't look like much to me. It is all dark."

"But of course. This, sir, is a negative image. In other words, what the eye sees as lighter shades and white registers on the negative in ebony hues, while the negative image of a lump of black anthracite will appear as a nugget of white alabaster."

I stared at the glass plate for a time, trying to make sense of the picture. "Well, what the hell good is that? Things ought to look more like what they are. Even if a regular picture is all gray and shows no color, at least it looks like what it is."

He smiled. "You speak the truth, my good man. The completion of the next step in the making of a photograph will, I say without fear of contradiction, fully satisfy your wish to see a more accurate representation of the world as visible to the eye."

He stepped back into the depths of the wagon, closed the door and hatch, opened a cupboard, and took out a flat box. Quick as he could, he slipped out a sheet of shiny paper and laid it behind the plate and slipped the whole of it into a frame like the one from the camera. He handed it to me, pushed open the hatch, and told me to hold it with the negative toward the sunlight. I handed him the frame after a bit and he looked it over, then held it out to the light for a little longer before again dropping the roof lid. He took the paper from the frame and slid it into a tray of juice to "fix" it. Even through the liquid as he rocked the tray back and forth, I could see a crisp, clear, picture of the windmill tower reaching into the sky, its shadow in the morning sun stretching toward the camera. The mountains and the saddleback pass stood sharp in the background. The sagebrush plain in between looked so clear you could not only see individual brush, but the branches on them as well.

"Well, I will be damned," I said. "That is my windmill, all right."

He washed the picture in water and clipped it to a string stretched near the ceiling. "Once it is dry, it is yours." He clapped a hand onto my shoulder. "Let us retire to the roadhouse. I should like to suggest to you a proposition that I believe will assay to our mutual benefit—after, of course, we have indulged in a cup of java, and perhaps a snack of whatever viands your good woman may have on hand."

Chapter Fourteen

Rather than simply eat a pickled egg by hand in a bite or two, the photographer asked for a plate and knife and fork. He carefully sliced his egg crosswise, and fanned the slices across the plate like a hand of playing cards. He forked up a slice and chewed it with his eyes closed.

"This white substance," he said, poking at a slice of egg with the tines of his fork. "Are you cognizant of its composition?"

"What?"

"Are you aware of what it is?"

I told him it was egg white. Everybody knows that.

"The Good Book, in the sixth verse of the sixth chapter of the Book of Job, poses a question: 'is there any taste in the white of an egg?' The query may be rhetorical, but the brining of this spawn of *Gallus domesticus* renders the question moot— the white of this egg certainly has taste—to the point of being rather delectable, I contend." He chewed another bite before continuing. "But, to my point. This," he said, again pointing at the white rim around the yellow yolk, "is a substance known as 'albumen,' one of a class of simple, sulfurous, water-soluble proteins that coagulate when heated."

"I guess that is interesting. But I am not sure why it should be."

He smiled and swallowed the bite he was chewing. "Albumen, this very substance," he said, again prodding a slice of egg with his fork, "is an integral constituent in the making of a photograph."

I did not respond, which seemed to dampen his spirits somewhat. But he pressed on, nevertheless.

"The photographs you handled this morning, and the one drying at present in the portable darkroom? You will recall they reside on paper? The surface of which, holding the image, is glossy?"

I nodded.

"That surface," he said, pointing his fork to the sky for emphasis, "is made lustrous owing to the presence of . . ." He paused, smiled, then said, "Albumen!"

He went on to say how those photographic sheets are made from high-quality cotton paper coated with an emulsion of egg white and sodium chloride—plain old salt, he said by way of translation—then dried and dipped in silver nitrate to make them sensitive to light. I shrugged. All in all, I thought, but did not say, I would as soon eat my albumen in peace.

After finishing his egg and a mug of coffee, he placed his palms on the tabletop. "And now, to business. Sir, I have a proposition for your consideration."

"And what might that be?"

"In lieu of recompense in specie for services rendered here at your establishment, may I suggest, rather, a photographic study of the roadhouse, its occupants, and the immediate vicinity?"

"You want to pay me with pictures instead of money?"

"You have, sir, correctly perceived my overture."

For reasons I cannot explain—call it a flight of fancy—I accepted his offer. I suppose the rarity of photographs in this country contributed to the decision. To have a picture of yourself and some of your surroundings seemed a valued possession.

We spent the rest of the day making photographs. Or, I should say, the photographer did. I did not care to watch him at work in the close confines and stink of the wagon. But I watched him stroll around as he composed the pictures in his mind, and position and reposition the camera on its tripod until satisfied. And I watched him run back and forth to the wagon to make the plates and hurry them back there afterward.

He took a picture of the woman standing just outside the roadhouse doorway. Her displeasure with it is evident in her expression in the photograph. He stood me between corrals in the alleyway leading to the barn. He photographed the barn and pens and outbuildings from various points of view.

In the late afternoon, the man who carried the mail came by and watched the goings-on for a time. I convinced him to sit horseback by the old rock well for a picture. His horse swished its tail at a fly, causing a blur, but it was an otherwise acceptable photograph.

Toward sundown, the photographer harnessed his mule and hitched it to the wagon and we drove out the road a ways toward the pass. After a few stops and starts he unhitched the mule, and I stood holding it while he hefted his camera and tripod atop the wagon and composed a picture of the whole place—the windmill and roadhouse and outbuildings and pens looking nice in the low light and shadows. I am convinced the place looks better in the picture than in real life.

We rattled back into the yard, and he penned the mule. The woman fed us a supper of bacon, beans, and biscuits, topped off with a dried-apple cobbler. The photographer ceased his otherwise ceaseless prattle as he shoveled the meal down his gullet like a man who had not eaten in recent memory. Then he carried on at length, telling the woman how the food was without equal and other such nonsense. It tasted pretty much like bacon and beans and biscuits always taste, if you ask me. The cobbler, however, was a welcome change. I would have to encourage the woman to make that more often.

We dickered for a time on the foodstuff and supplies coming

to him in the trade, and I set aside a pile of goods for him on the counter. Afterward, the photographer sat up talking until late—I would say *we* sat up talking, but I do not recall contributing more than a few *hmm*s, and *aahh*s, and nods of the head to the conversation. About the third time he prodded me awake with a poke of his finger, he must have decided we were finished talking. He retired to his wagon, where I suppose he rolled out a blanket on the darkroom floor. I pushed the bedroom doorway curtain aside and sat on the edge of the bed listening to the woman snore for a few minutes, then pulled off my boots and unslung my braces, undressed, and crawled into bed.

I slept through breakfast the next morning. A night of restful sleep is so rare that I made it last as long as possible. The woman fed the photographer, and he drove off. I suppose I should have rolled out to tell him goodbye and thank him for his custom. But I did not care to listen to any more of his fancy talk, so my guilt was not sufficient to stir me from my slumber.

He left the photographs he had made on the table. I spent what was left of the morning sipping coffee and studying them in great detail. Like I said, they somehow made things look better than what they are.

The peace and quiet around the place after the photographer left was a relief. I did not realize how much he talked until silence replaced his ceaseless chatter. Not that I regretted his having been here—the photographs he left behind lent hours of pleasure. I even cobbled together some backing and frames from the lumber pile and hung them on the walls. All except the picture of the woman. Every time I hung it up, she took it down and put it face down on a shelf. If not for my promise of punishment, I believe she would have destroyed it. I finally succumbed to her wishes, however, and put the picture in the trunk.

I took the opportunity to check the stash under the false bottom. Since the money from the bank robbery had fallen into my hands, there was enough there—and buried elsewhere—to set me up for life. I could get out of this isolated hell hole and take up residence in a more favorable location and live a life of leisure. Still, I could not fault the roadhouse for providing the means to a better life. Is that not why we all labor? To attain the means to better ourselves? Showing hospitality to travelers, along with taking advantage of other opportunities that revealed themselves, had provided a comfortable existence. And, now, the cached rewards would provide even more comfort for all the years yet to come.

Over the years, I had accumulated a considerable number of maps. Most depicted the United States, but a handful showed other places—Canada, Mexico, Europe, South America, even a map of the Hawaiian Islands. I often spread a map on the table for study, contemplating the many places my money could take me. It was not an easy decision. The old stage station, after all, had been home to me far longer than any other place of residence. And I had suffered less misfortune here. I would by no means call it the long-sought-for "happy home" of fairy tale and fantasy, but I had found a certain contentment.

Some may question my means of making a living here. But my actions do not disturb my sleep, at least to my knowledge—there are nightmares enough to occupy my dreams without concerning myself as to their origin. Besides, a man is entitled to all he can get his hands on. If it comes at the expense of others, well, so be it. The Golden Rule aside, I have found more profit in first doing unto others what they would do unto me if given half a chance. The bones in the well never cry my name. At least not that I have ever heard.

One day a few weeks after the visit from the photographer, a man rode in from the east. He rode an ordinary-looking bay horse and led an unremarkable packhorse. But strung on a line behind the packhorse were two leggy sorrel horses showing breeding not common in this country. Their slick hides glistened, their hooves were trimmed and well-shod, manes and tails flowing and glowing. It was obvious the cowboy took pride in the two horses. One looked to stand about sixteen hands, the other a hand higher. The smaller of the two was a gelding with a blaze face and four white socks; the taller a studhorse with no markings save a small star on its forehead. As I said, both were sorrels—a rich, deep shade some call chestnut.

The cowboy stepped down at the trough at the windmill. He was compact in size but moved with the confidence of a bigger man. He first led the sorrels to water and did not complain when I mentioned the cost. Then he watered his mount and the packhorse and inquired about a meal and a place to spend the night.

He supped on venison stew and boiled rice, cornbread, and bottled beer. I offered coffee afterward, but he said he only drank coffee in the morning, as it kept him awake at night if he drank it any later in the day.

"I'd have another bottle of that beer if you've got any," he said.

I fetched him one, then sat down opposite with my coffee. "That is some fine-looking horseflesh out there. Not your ordinary cow ponies. They look to be big, strong horses."

He nodded. "Mostly what they are is fast."

"You mean as in racing?"

"I mean just that." He sucked a long drink from the bottle and wiped the residue from his mouth with a shirtsleeve. "See, I been racin' all over Colorado and Kansas. Won me a fair-size poke. But word gets around, you know, and I can't get up a match anywhere in that country no more."

I said nothing, figuring he would go on with his story if there was more to tell. After another drink, which emptied the bottle, he asked for another. He sampled the brew in that one and started talking again.

"What I aim to do is go on over Californy way. They got lots of horses over there, and they ain't too shy 'bout runnin' 'em. Or so I'm told." He drank again. "See, these horses come out of Kentucky. Thoroughbreds. They was born to run. Ain't no Californy horses can keep up with 'em. Leastways that's my way of thinkin'." He drank again, holding on to the bottle afterward and tracing his finger through the wet ring it had left on the tabletop. "And I'm willin' to back that up with any kind of bet them folks over there wants to make."

I brought him another beer. "Seems like horses like that would cost a man a pretty penny."

He allowed as how they would but offered no clue as to how they came into his possession. The cowboy did not strike me as the son of a rich planter, or even having come from Kentucky or Tennessee or anywhere else back that way. But how he came by the animals was his business, not mine.

We talked some more, and he asked about buying a sack of feed grain for the Thoroughbreds, and some provisions for himself. While I put together a sack of canned goods and coffee and flour and salt and sugar, he looked over the pictures on the wall.

"I seen this fellow," he said, standing before the photograph of the man who carries the mail. "Passed him on the road."

"He comes by here now and again. Takes mail over to the mining towns in the mountains—what is left of them—and picks up any letters they want to send." I told the cowboy how much he owed, and he paid the bill without complaint. "The oats are out in the barn. I will sack some up for you and bring it by your camp."

Grasping the bag of food supplies by the twisted and tied top, he slung it over his shoulder and headed out the door. I followed him, went on to the barn, and scooped out what I figured to be the amount of oats he wanted, then added a bit more for good measure. Then, much as he had done with his grub sack, I slung the tied bag over my shoulder and carried it out to where he had spread his bedroll, next to the corral where his four horses were penned. He sat on the tarp cover of his bed, pulling off his boots, and waved me over to where his packsaddle lay, the panniers and what all he had to fill them with piled beside. I added the sack of grain to the collection.

"There will be hot coffee in the morning," I told him. "And the woman will fix you up with some breakfast."

He was rolling a cigarette and only nodded in reply. I wished him a good night and walked back to the roadhouse.

Hours later, awakened by a forgotten but troublesome dream, I walked back outside. As I passed the woodshed, I picked up the axe and used it to split the sleeping cowboy's skull like so much stove wood.

The sheen of lamplight on puddles, like irregular mirrors dropped in the mud. The boy stood at the end of the street. Glowing windows line the roadway, dimming into the distance. No one about, driven indoors by rain no longer falling. He chose the right-hand side, picked a path through pools of standing water, and stepped onto the boardwalk. He thought he remembered someone once saying that if you do not know where you are going it does not matter much which way you go.

He had not passed more than two cross streets when a man stepped out of the dark recess of a doorway and asked the boy what he sought. Then offered to guide him to just such a place. When the man turned into a soggy passageway between two buildings, the boy followed.

The boy had no more than stepped from the narrow lane into the back alley when he was grabbed by each arm. His guide turned and struck him with a walking stick. Breath burst from his lungs as fists pummeled his belly from both sides. The boy collapsed to his knees, wheezing as he fought for air. The long arc of the walking stick's stroke ended just above his ear, and he fell into the fetid sludge.

They took his coat. His shoes, taken from his feet. The thugs pilfered his pockets, leaving nothing of value. His valise plundered, unwanted baggage trampled into the mire. He lay helpless, benumbed by agony and distress, as they pried apart shirttail and waistband to expose the money belt.

The boy managed to roll to his side. He drew up his knees and folded his arms about his head as boot blows landed and landed some more, long after he knew anything of it.

CHAPTER FIFTEEN

I pulled off the cowboy's boots and spurs and undressed him, setting aside what looked useful and tossing the rest onto the bloody bedroll cover. Rolling him in the canvas sheet with the ruined clothes, I lifted the small man over my shoulder and carried him to the old well. I draped him over the rock rim and sat down to catch my breath, then stood and dumped him over the side, waiting for the sound of his bottoming out in the depths.

There looked to be a hint of dawn in the eastern sky. I gathered the cowboy's gear and goods and put them in a dark corner of the barn, threw his pack cover over them, then forked a cover of hay over the pile. I saddled the old mare, haltered the two racehorses, and set off in the growing light for the canyon. The cowboy's other horses—his mount and pack animal—would not seem out of place in my pens, but the big sorrels would draw unwanted notice. Truth be told, I had no idea what I would do with them. Perhaps the commander or one of the officers at the fort would be interested in a showy mount. In any case, spending time in the canyon would soon wear the polish off their well-brushed hides, and while that would not put them on a par with ordinary horses, they would stand out a little less.

At the canyon, I tied the old mare to the cottonwood tree by the cabin and pulled the shoes off the sorrels. The shoes did not show much wear, so I stuffed them in my saddlebags and mounted the mare and started for home. The sun was well up, and my stomach reminded me I had missed breakfast.

The cowboy's purchases went back into the grain bin and onto the store shelves. His saddle was a stripped-down affair, likely to reduce its weight for racing. I couldn't see any use for it, so down the well it went. The packsaddle and panniers might find a buyer, so I added them to my supply. The "poke" the cowboy mentioned he had earned racing was in leather pouches made to fit in the bottom of each of those panniers, gold coins evenly divided between them to distribute the weight. A few rolls of paper money were also tucked into each pouch. With no room in the trunk, the cash went into the other cache that only I knew.

By the time I finished, I had missed dinner as well. I stopped at the washstand and scrubbed off the grime, wondering if soap would help remove the blood from the creases around my fingernails. But, as always, there was no soap on the washstand. The woman eyed me with a blend of curiosity and coolness when I went in. I told her I was hungry and to fix something quick. She fried some ham and scrambled up some eggs, and put out a plate of yesterday's cornbread. Washed down with coffee, the meal satisfied my hunger.

The road saw no traffic for many a day. Then one evening the man who carried the mail rode in. He complained about the cost of a drink of water, as usual. He asked about a meal and said he intended to stay over. After watering his horse, and before coming inside, he rode over to old well as he often did. He again stood in one stirrup and leaned over the rim. You would think he would realize someday that a well that deep revealed nothing. As he unsaddled his horse, he took his time about it, studying the wagons in the yard, the parts and equipment, the stock in the pens and pasture.

I went on inside and left him to his snooping. After a time, I heard him splashing around in the wash basin outside the door.

He came in and ate, then came over to the counter and asked for a glass of rye whiskey. He downed the first in a gulp, and I poured the second.

"Somethin' about this stuff cuts the trail dust better than water," he said. "Better than coffee, even." This time, he sipped the drink slowly. "On my last trip, goin' over east, I passed a man leadin' two sorrel horses. Fancy-lookin' horses. Didn't look like they'd be much good for workin' cows. My guess is they was racehorses."

"That is what he said when he came by here," I said.

The man acknowledged what I said with his half nod. "Stopped over, then, did he?"

I shrugged. "Only for water." I topped off his glass. "Did not complain about the cost, either—like some will do."

He smiled a half smile and sipped his drink. The room was growing darker, closing in on the glow from the lantern on the table, so I struck a match and lit another lamp and set it at the end of the counter—or bar, given its present purpose. The man finished the drink. I walked around the counter and picked up the light as I passed.

"Come along over here," I said. "There is something you should see."

I led him over to the pictures on the wall and lifted the light to illuminate the photograph of the man on his horse. I could not see his reaction, as he stood more or less in front of me. He studied it for a while.

"That's me all right," he said. "What's the matter there with the horse's hind end?"

I stepped around him and waggled my finger by the horse's tail. "See here—that is the tail swishing at a fly, or something, just as the photographer opened up the camera. He says things that move get blurred like that. He used some highfalutin words to explain it, but that is what it comes down to. Everything has to stay still when a picture is taken."

He gave that little half nod and looked at the photograph some more. "How come you to put me by that old well for the picture?"

I smiled. "Seems like you like to spend time there. One of these days, you will lean off your horse to look in and lose your balance and fall down that hole."

"It could happen, I reckon. But at least then I'd know what the hell's down there that smells so bad most all the time."

He smiled in the glow of the lantern and asked to take it. I handed it over, and he stood by the wall looking over the photographs one by one.

"I don't see no picture of your woman—your wife."

"He did one of her, but she does not want it seen."

"No more than she wants to be seen herself, I guess," he said. "Never been around a woman so shy as she is."

The man handed me the lantern and said he would settle up tonight, as he wanted to get an early start come the morning. Said he would kindle a fire outside and boil some coffee on his own. He stopped at the door to say he had passed the freighter on the road, and that he had something on his wagon for me and would likely be along tomorrow.

When I woke up in the morning the sun was yet a long way from showing its face, but the mail carrier was gone and the buried ashes of his fire barely warm to the touch.

The freighter did come by later in the day. He bypassed the trough and stopped the wagon near the roadhouse door. I watched him drop the tailgate and step up into the box—not an easy thing, given that goods were stacked right to the back of the wagon, leaving but a narrow ledge on which to stand. He shifted a gunnysack off the top of the stacks and, in one motion, swung it free, turned, and lowered to the ground.

"Onions," he said.

He pulled down a larger sack.

"Spuds—Irish potatoes."

Then, a smaller sack, similar in size to the one holding onions.

"Carrots."

That was about all I expected, but one more sack came off the stacks.

"Turnips."

Then, from another stack, a box. That, he lowered to the ledge of the wagon's floor and balanced it there as he jumped off the wagon and set the box on the ground.

"Apples."

That was a surprise. And, a pleasant one. I tried my best not to signal my pleasure. I looked over the goods, opening the mouth of the carrot sack. I picked out a carrot, brushed the dirt off, and took a bite. It tasted sweet, as well as bitter. Everything looked as good as could be expected, given its long ride across the desert. It had been some time since anything occupied the root cellar, and this stuff should keep well once deposited in the cool and dark.

The freighter tipped back his strange hat and hooked his thumbs in the bib of his overalls. "I reckon that more than covers the cost of you keepin' my ox."

I feigned skepticism. "I don't know. He has been in my care for quite a spell. I suppose you already know that that animal has a healthy appetite."

"Still and all, what I got here, and the way I got skinned on the price of the ox you sold me—well, I'd say we're more than square."

After a lengthy bout of what looked to be deep thought and calculation, I concurred.

He unhitched his thumbs, smiled, and said, "By the by—is that ox fit to travel?"

"Oh, he will be by the time you get back here. If I were you, I would not put him under yoke as yet. But he should be able to trail along behind the wagon without difficulty."

"You'll keep him till I come by goin' home, then—without another bill?"

"I will. In fact, I will overlook the charge for drinking at the windmill."

He snorted. "Well, hell, that's mighty generous of you."

The scornful nature of his remark tempted me to withdraw the offer, but I thought better of it. "I take it they have another load of ore for you at the mines."

"Some. Don't know as it'll fill the wagon. Don't know if there'll be another. But, they always seem to scrape together enough pay dirt to make it worth hauling out. And some of them miners is always believin' there's a big vein of gold there just waitin' to be discovered." He lifted his hat and mopped the top of his head with a grimy handkerchief. He shook his head. "It's a far cry from the way it used to be out there, that's for damn sure. Used to be freight wagons goin' back and forth on this road ever' day. Stagecoaches, too. Now, there ain't enough traffic to keep the weeds out of the road. And without no maintenance, a man has to keep a sharp lookout he don't bust a wheel or axle on a rock, or in a pothole."

He mopped his head again. "Well, I'd best be on my way. Ain't no profit standin' here complainin' to the likes of you."

The freighter turned the double yoke of oxen and the wagon back onto the road. With the goad laying on his shoulder, he turned back and said, "I'll take you up on that free water on the way home. Watered 'em up good this mornin' from the barrels."

I went inside and told the woman to get the vegetables and the apples into the root cellar and to be quick about it. I sat down with a mug of coffee, thick and bitter from sitting on the stove since morning. Still, I drank it. Coffee came too dear to allow it to go to waste. As I sat and thought, I decided to have the woman butcher a steer. I could almost taste beef roasted in a cast-iron pot, with onions and carrots and potatoes soaking in the juices. Yes, I thought. I will have the woman do just that. And I will make sure she does not waste any time getting it done.

By the time the woman killed, cooled, and cut up the steer, the hunger in my mind and mouth was all but overwhelming. The food she fixed in the interim seemed insipid, even though it was the normal kind of fare I routinely ate, and while I did not exactly enjoy it, it served its purpose. As it happened, the man who carried the mail came back through the day the woman pulled the pot out of the oven. The dinner placed before him that afternoon should have set him back more than the normal fifty cents.

Between the two of us, we consumed more of the savory meat and vegetables than we should have, keeping our knives and forks working until we reached the point of discomfort. Even the biscuits that sopped up the brothy residue puddled on our plates seemed tastier than usual. We waved off the notion of coffee or beer or whiskey after the meal, our distended stomachs unable to accommodate even the thought of it.

The mail carrier pushed back from the table, belched, excused himself, and belched again. He pulled a matchstick and a clasp knife from his vest pockets, carved a sharp point onto the stick, and set to picking his teeth. Satisfied after several minutes' prodding and sucking at his teeth, he propped one booted foot on the opposite knee and talked.

He commented on the quality of the meal. He mentioned he had passed the freighter, still plodding along on the way to the mines. Then he put his foot down, leaned forward, and propped his elbows on the tabletop.

"Odd thing," he said. "You remember that cowboy with them two good-lookin' sorrel horses? The one I passed comin' this way? You said he stopped by here and bought some supplies."

I nodded but said nothing.

He insisted. "You remember the one I mean?"

"Yes. I remember. What about it?"

"Well, here's the thing. I talked to folks in them towns at the mines. Wasn't a one of 'em said anything about seein' them horses."

I shrugged. "Maybe they were not paying attention."

"Oh, I don't think so. Horses like them two is pretty hard to miss. Even if you don't know a whole lot about horses, you could see they was somethin' special."

"Maybe they saw them but saw no need to mention it to you."

He shook his head. "Can't be that. It struck me as odd, so I asked some of 'em right out if they had seen a cowboy leadin' a pack horse and two other horses come through there. Not a one of 'em saw any such thing."

I thought for a minute. "Maybe he decided to go cross-country and left the road somewhere."

After a bit, he gave me that half nod of his. "I suppose that's possible. But I can't see him doin' that. Not when the road gets him over the mountains the best way there is."

"But he would not know that, would he?"

He only looked at me. And looked.

I leaned forward in my chair until he could probably smell the onions on my breath. "Listen, mister, are you accusing me of something?"

He sat upright. "No. Not at all." He stood. "Just curious, that's all." He tossed a dollar coin on the table. "I'll be on my way. Here's for the meal and the water. Give the extra to your woman. Can't say when I last had a meal good as that one."

He stopped after opening the door and turned and looked

back at me long enough to make me squirm a little, if only inside.

"Just curious," he said. "Somehow, it don't make sense."

CHAPTER SIXTEEN

A few days later the freighter came back through. He led his lame ox out of the corral and walked it around, watching for any sign of weakness in the injured hoof. The ox still favored it a bit, but the wound had healed with no sign of corruption. The freighter lifted the leg and poked and prodded in and all around the hoof. The ox flinched when he nudged the cloven area where the wound had been, but tenderness would be expected.

He determined the beast fit to travel and tacked on fresh shoes all around. With evening well on the way, he decided to stay over the night. I told him hot food was available inside, but he said he could fend for himself and would. And he reminded me of my offer for free use of water from the trough.

The world was a deep, faded gray when I awoke from a disturbed sleep. I pulled on my britches and boots and stepped out to visit the backhouse. The freighter was already up and about, silhouetted against his campfire as he packed up his gear and stowed it on and in the Murphy wagon. By the time I finished my business, he had his wheelers yoked and was bringing the lead team back from the windmill trough. The lame ox was already tied to the back of the wagon with a lead rope also fashioned into a makeshift halter. He saw me watching.

"I already watered the stock. I'll fill my kegs and be on my way."

With a mug of yesterday's coffee warming my hands, I sat on the roadhouse steps and watched the wagon cross the sagebrush flat and climb the long, easy slant up to the saddleback pass and disappear over the top. The sun had yet to rise, but as he reached the summit the wagon cover glowed in the coming rays.

I smelled cooking and went inside. The woman had potatoes and onions frying in one skillet and bacon and fried eggs sizzling in the another. There was also a fresh pot of coffee and sliced bread toasting on the stovetop. I refilled my mug and sat at the table waiting for her to dish up my breakfast. I savored the spuds and onions especially. The deal with the freighter proved itself a smart bargain with every bite. Even in soup, desiccated vegetables did not measure up to the real thing.

It was quiet on the road for several days. Then, late one afternoon, visitors came by. Visitors the like of which I had never seen before. Children.

Oh, not that I had not seen children on the road before, but, in those instances, they were in the company of family. At least I supposed them to be family. But the children were certainly in the company of adults. These were not.

They came laboring along the road from the west with a two-wheeled cart pulled by a wasted claybank pony. The scrawny horse was emaciated to the point it looked as much like a skinned hide draped over a rack of bones while wet and left to dry. His eyes were rheumy and crusted, his ears droopy, his hoofs chipped and cracked, his mane and tail tangled and embedded with burs. Limping along behind the cart came a mongrel dog, looking as much like a twin to the pony as possible for a dog and horse to look alike.

A half-grown, shoeless girl in tattered clothes walked beside the horse. Beside the cart stumbled a ragged boy who looked to be a year or two younger. Sitting in the cart, or, rather, kneeling in the cart with hands on the sideboards, was a small girl watching me through eyes that seemed to see beyond where she looked.

I walked out to the road to meet them. When the cart drew near, the older girl stopped. The pony, unbidden, stopped when she did, as did the boy. The dog dropped to his belly where he stood, his neck stretched out and lower jaw in the dirt. The little girl in the cart watched me.

It took me a few minutes of staring until words spilled out. "What are you children doing away out here? Where are you going? Where are your folks?"

The older girl looked from me to the windmill, then back to me. "Could we trouble you for a drink of water, mister? We're right thirsty."

I nodded, and she grabbed the patched-together cheek piece on the pony's bridle and tugged, and the little horse stumbled into motion and walked beside her to the trough. The boy and dog followed as well. The horse buried its head in the trough almost to its eyes and sucked in water. The girl took the tin cup from the nail on the windmill frame, filled it from the pipe, and took it to the younger girl. She refilled it for herself, then the boy. As the boy drank, she fetched a dented-up tin cooking pot from the cart and dipped it into the trough, filling it for the dog. She took the cup from the boy, filled it from the pipe, and they passed it around again.

While they drank, I stepped near the cart. The little girl never took her eyes off me as I studied the contents of the box, which were few. A scattering of pots and pans, dented and rusted and looking for all the world like refugees from a trash heap. A rumpled stack of threadbare blankets and quilts. A few sacks and bags, with heaven-knows-what inside. There was no trace of food or water, save a small puddle, barely more than a wet spot, in a pan tipped nearly on its side.

I turned to the girl. "Don't you have anything to eat?"

She stepped to the cart and opened one of the sacks, showing me the contents. Inside was a jumble of hardtack, which struck me as surplus from the long-ago War Between the States. Where it came from, or how it came to be with the children, seemed a farfetched mystery. Most of the crackers were broken, and others were no more than dust in the creases and bottom of the sack.

"You eat that stuff?"

She lifted her nose in the air. "If'n you soak it some in water, it ain't so bad."

"Is that all you have?"

The girl rolled the mouth of the sack closed and opened another. She reached in and came out with a stick of dried meat. "We got some of this." She gestured with her chin toward the road they had traveled. "Some Indians back yonderway give it to us."

"Come with me."

I started for the roadhouse, and the girl turned the horse and cart to follow. I waited near the door for them to catch up. I told the girl to get herself and the others washed up. I went inside and came back with a cake of soap, unwrapped it, and tossed it into the washbowl. "This will help get you cleaned up. When you are finished, come on inside."

After telling the woman to cook plenty of food, and quickly, I went back outside. I told the girl I would unhitch the cart and take care of her horse. When I came back, the children were at the table with their faces in their plates. The woman had stirred up a batch of flapjacks and drizzled them with molasses. She had bacon frying and was scrambling eggs in another skillet. All three of the children ate in earnest, looking up from their plates only when empty, to plead with their eyes for more food. They ate so much I feared they might founder. The edge finally off their appetites, the children sat up in their chairs and looked around. I gave them a few minutes to satisfy their curiosity, then sat down at the table with them.

The boy spoke for the first time. "That there Injun woman ain't said a word. Can't she talk none?"

Rather than explain, I simply said no. I asked the girl where they came from.

"Over at the mines. Back yonder in the mountains."

"Why did you leave?"

She shrugged. "Couldn't stay there no longer. We'd of starved."

"What about your folks?"

"Ain't got none."

"How is that?"

She thought for a time. "They're all dead. Papa, he got killed by a rock fall in the mine long time ago. Mama, she died some months back. Got the consumption and couldn't do nothin' about it." Her eyes were moist, but she held back the tears. She shrugged. "She died."

After their father died, she said their mother cooked for a time in an eating house until it closed down, then took in washing and "did other things." But then she got too sick, and one cold morning did not wake up.

"We got by best as we could. But there weren't no way for us to get any money for food. Beggin' for food ain't right, Mama and Papa always said. Some of them folks livin' 'round there helped us some—most of them wasn't much better off than we was. Lots of folks leavin' out of there. Even them that still had work was bad off, 'cept for the ones what run the mines. Papa and Mama always said those people didn't care none 'bout workin' folks. Long as they made their money, they didn't care none if them what done the work lived or died."

Now a tear rolled down her cheek, and she wiped it away with the back of her hand and sniffled. "Near as I can tell, that's the truth."

She told me she was fourteen years old, her brother twelve, and the little girl six. The cart they had found dumped in a ravine outside the town and had only to nail on one sideboard and mend one of the shafts to make it serviceable. The wheels were rickety but had held up so far. The pony was likewise abandoned, found by the boy wandering the hills and ridges around the town. He had followed and watched it for several days, to make sure it did not belong to someone who might accuse them of stealing it. As for the dog, it had just followed them out of town and stayed with them ever since. They thought it must have been abandoned, too—like all of them, and all they carried.

Through it all, the little girl did not speak. She only watched.

I told the woman to make up some sleeping pallets on the floor for the children. I sat on the step with a mug of coffee sweetened with rum and watched the day fade into night.

When I woke up next morning, the woman was gone from the bed. I dressed and pushed aside the curtain and saw that the children, too, were up and about. I joined the boy and little girl at the table, and the woman put a plate of biscuits smothered with gravy stirred up from bacon grease and flour and canned milk in front of me.

The older girl's chair was pulled away from the table. After serving my breakfast, the woman went back to what she had been doing there. The girl had her dress hiked up to her knees, and the woman knelt before her, rubbing some kind of oil or liniment or something into her feet. Heavily callused and scarred, her feet were lined with creases and cracks, some red from dried blood, others black with grime. The woman worked over the boy's feet next. The little girl's feet were not so battered and bruised, as she had spent most of the trip riding in the cart, but they, too, were hard and scaly from lack of shoes for who knows how long.

I went to the store shelves and pawed through clothing I had collected from passing wagons and found some stockings that looked like they might fit the children. They were worn but with plenty of wear left in them. Then I pulled out a gunnysack filled with shoes and boots and dumped it out on the floor. There were few shoes of a size to fit children, but each of them managed to find a pair that fit, or close enough.

"Later on, we will see what we can find in the way of clothes," I said. "Now, there is work to do outside. Come along."

Outside the door, the mongrel dog lay working over a bone the woman must have put out for him. The woman took the little girl by the hand and took her to check the henhouse for eggs, and to accompany her as she carried water to the stock and forked them some hay. I took the girl and boy to where I had parked their cart.

I walked around and around the cart, looking it over, shaking it, lifting the shafts, and rocking it back and forth. "You say you fixed up this cart?"

The girl and boy nodded in unison.

"You did a workmanlike job. I see where you reinforced this cracked shaft with wire and rawhide. And this repair you made on the box—the board you put in fits nicely." The truth was, the cart was a ramshackle affair and could have collapsed into a heap at any time.

I said, "The wheels are suspect, however." I grasped the top of one wheel and shifted it from side to side. "You see that?" They nodded. "Now, you want some play in a wheel, but this is too much." I showed them how some of the spokes were loose, and one cracked near to breaking.

The boy swallowed hard and looked ready to cry. "We didn't have no other way to fix it," he said, hanging his head and tracing a path back and forth in the dirt with the toe of his shoe.

The girl, on the other hand, was red faced and scowling. "He did the best he could!"

I raised a hand. "No, no. I meant no disrespect. As I said before, your work on the cart shows initiative and skill. And, truth is, wheels are complicated in their workmanship. Few can repair them properly, outside a wheelwright trained and equipped for it."

I made another round or two of the cart, checking it further. Then, "Come with me." The children followed me to a small buckboard I had acquired quite some time ago. Its paint had long since peeled away, and the wood was dry and brittle in places for want of protection. But, none of the buckboard's faults would affect its ability to travel. I circled the wagon as I had the cart, pointing out to the children its works.

"The thing is," I said when finished, "this particular buckboard is of no use to me. I have been unable to sell it, owing to its small size. Most people who need a wagon are looking for something more substantial. At the same time, it is too large for hauling things around the place, here. What I really need for that work is a cart—a two-wheeled affair, much like that one of yours."

I looked at the children, and they looked at me. They seemed unsure as to what I was up to. "What would you say to a trade? Straight across—this buckboard for your cart?"

I expected delight. Instead, the girl looked troubled and the boy confused. I asked them if my offered buckboard was insufficient for a trade.

"No, mister," the girl said. "But that there pony of ours, well, he can't barely pull that cart. Ain't no way he could pull this thing. It'd be too heavy for him."

I smiled. "Is that all? Look here." I turned and walked to the big corral. "As you see, I have draft animals available. Now, an ox would not serve your purposes. But look at that little brown mule over in the corner. The one looking this way. I believe he would serve you well. He is not young, mind you—I would put his age at about thirteen years. You, of course, are free to check his mouth and make your own determination."

The girl said, "We don't know nothin' 'bout what's in a mule's mouth."

I smiled. "Well, then. I guess you will have to take my word for it."

"Papa said you can't never believe one damn thing a horse trader tells you," the boy said.

"Your papa was a wise man."

"Besides," the girl said, "we ain't got nothin' to buy no mule with."

"Buy? Who said anything about buy? I am talking trade here. Your horse for my mule. Now, of course it is in no way an equal trade. Your pony is emaciated and in poor health, whereas the mule is in peak condition. You have no cash to offer as boot in the trade. But, if you are willing, I would allow you to make up the difference in labor."

They looked at one another, each seeing in the other's face a reflection of fear and uncertainty.

"Well," I said, "think it over. We do not have to come to terms just now. We will wait until tomorrow. By then, the picture of what lies in store may become clear."

We started back to the roadhouse, anxiety and disquiet accompanying the children.

Chapter Seventeen

We idled away the rest of the day. The children needed the rest, and it was likely the first day in many for them with sufficient food and drink at hand. Still, the girl looked worried. I suspect she feared there was obligation attached to the room and board. The boy seemed more suspicious than worried, but for the same reason, I believed. The little girl stayed close to the woman. She seemed comfortable in the silence they shared.

The boy, though tired out till near exhaustion, was nonetheless restless. He wandered the roadhouse, looking anywhere and everywhere at anything and everything. Not once did his fingers touch anything, however. Finally, his wandering took him to the photographs on the wall.

"Hey!" he said, pointing at the picture the photographer took from atop his wagon. "That there is this place!"

The girl hurried over to stand beside him. They studied the other photographs, recognizing in some of them buildings and corrals in the yard. And, of course, the windmill. They looked at the picture of the letter carrier.

"We seen that man," the girl said. "We seen him comin' through town now 'n then."

"He carries letters for people," I said. "Brings them mail, and takes letters to post."

The girl shook her head. "We ain't never got no mail."

"How come you to have these here pictures?" the boy said.

I told them how a photographer had come by and made

146

them. When I described his wagon, they recalled seeing it around their town, but, as with the letter carrier, they had no notion of its reason for being.

"Papa, he had a picture," the boy said.

I said nothing, waiting to see if there was more to the story.

"It weren't like these ones. It was little. Made out of tin. He kep' it in a little leather billfold."

This time, I did not wait, but asked what was in the picture.

"It was a picture of Mama. 'Fore ever we knew her. She was a purty girl when that picture got took."

"Did you keep it after your father died?"

The girl sighed. "No. Papa kep' it with him always. Had it with him when he got buried in the mine."

"I can't hardly see their faces no more," the boy said. "I'm scairt I'll forget how they looked. They's just . . . gone."

The woman fed us a dinner of sliced ham with beans and mashed turnips and cornbread. The little girl followed her everywhere, holding fast to her skirts and watching everything she did. The woman even let her help when there was a job a girl of her size could do.

Afterward, I rolled out a map on the table. I showed the girl and boy where the mountains and mining towns were and traced the old stage road from there to the roadhouse. There was little showing on the map for inches in every direction from where we sat, save range after range of mountains and the intervening valleys. It was several days' journey to the rim of the basin. But, there, towns of various sizes and even a fair-sized city were tucked along the edge of a lengthy mountain range. They examined the map and seemed to make some sense of it.

"See how far you have come to get to this place," I said, again tracing the road. "Now, see how far it is until you get to where people live." They could see it was farther than they had already traveled. "Oh, there are some people living along the way, on cattle and sheep ranches here and there. But not many, and not always on the road. And it is a long way between water. And many a day goes by when there is no one traveling the road."

I let that sink in for a few minutes as they stared at the map and its emptiness. "Where is it you intend to go?"

After a minute, the girl sniffled. "We don't have nowheres to go. We just knowed we couldn't stay where we was." She ran her finger along the string of settlements at the other end of the basin. "If we could get over there, where there's people, we might could find some kind of work and a place to stay. I can do housework. Cook some, but not much. I could learn. My brother, he's handy and can do most any job of work if he's give a chance."

I rolled up the map and put it back in the box with others of its kind. "Not only is it a long road to get to the settlements, as you have seen, it is a hard one. There are mountain passes to negotiate, and the road is not as well maintained as it was when the stagecoaches ran. But, with careful driving, wrecks and breakdowns can usually be avoided. There is little danger from Indians—but there are Indians about, and some will do you harm if they see profit in it." That speech did little to allay their downcast looks. I asked the boy if he could shoot.

"I ain't never shot no gun," he said, shaking his head. "A kid I used to know, 'fore he moved away, he sometimes snuck his daddy's rifle out of the house. We make-believe shot it, but not never for real."

"Well, that is one thing easily enough remedied," I said. "Come along."

He followed me back among the store shelves. Several long guns were propped in a corner—rifles, carbines, shotguns of various makes and models. Even a couple of old muzzle load-ers. For some of the guns, I did not even have ammunition. On nearby shelves was a similar selection of handguns. I looked through the long guns and pulled a Winchester Yellow Boy carbine out of the stack. Like the others, it was a gun I had acquired from travelers on the road, either in trade or otherwise. It was a valuable rifle, but I figured it would be easy for a boy of his size to handle.

I found a box of .44-caliber rimfire cartridges and handed it and the rifle to the boy and told him to follow me. On the way past the counter, I picked up a powder box of empty beer and whiskey bottles. Telling the boy to wait in the yard, I carried the box out to the old well and lined up a row of bottles along the rock wall rim.

When I got back, the boy held the rifle crosswise, studying how it was put together, and tracing its parts with a finger. I let him hold it and pointed out the parts fundamental to its operation.

I said, "This is a Winchester rifle—carbine, really, on account of its length, which is shorter than the proper rifle. Folks call it the 'Yellow Boy,' and I imagine you can see why."

He rubbed his hand over the brass receiver and said, "This right here?"

I nodded and showed him the loading gate and let him press it down with his thumb to get a feel for how it worked, and explained how the cartridges slid into the magazine tube. "The magazine holds thirteen bullets, which lets you fire more and faster, and reload quicker, than most any other gun." I rolled the rifle over and back to show him the cartridge lifter and elevator and warned him to keep his fingers away from them when shooting.

He grinned and looked up at me. "You mean I can shoot it?"

"Soon enough. Now," I said, "grab hold of that lever and pull it down."

With some hesitation and a little effort, he worked the lever to open the chamber. I stopped him to point out how the inner workings would lift a cartridge and how the bolt cocked the hammer, then how, when he lifted the lever, the chamber would close, and the bolt would push the cartridge into position. I let him squeeze the trigger to get a feel for it and showed him how to cock and release the hammer with his thumb. Then I showed him how to shoulder the rifle and use the leaf and front sights to aim. Finally, I showed him how to twist the "safety" and lock the lever against the stock when the gun was not in use.

"Do you understand?"

He grinned and nodded, and I tested him on a few points. The boy obviously had his wits about him, for he answered my questions quickly and correctly. Through all this, the girl stood by and watched. She said nothing, but I had the feeling she had comprehended every word and action.

I took the rifle and pushed a couple of cartridges through the gate, then handed it back to the boy and watched him fumble around until he got the hang of it. I retrieved the Winchester, said, "Pay attention, boy," and jacked the lever. I snugged the butt plate against my shoulder. "See the brown bottle there on the well?" I suspect he nodded, but I asked him again and he answered.

"Watch." I squeezed the trigger and could see out of the corner of my eye the boy and girl flinch at the sound. The bottle burst into a thousand fragments. The boy looked at me and grinned again. I handed him the rifle. "You try it."

Still smiling, he put the rifle to his shoulder and moved it back and forth until comfortable. The barrel weaved and dipped as he grew accustomed to its weight and balance. He squeezed the trigger. He squeezed it again, with more pressure. It did not move. "It don't work!"

"What did you forget to do?"

He looked at me with a question of his own in his eyes, but I did not answer.

"You didn't work that lever," the girl said.

The boy's face reddened. He let the buttstock drop from his shoulder and propped it on his thigh for support as he worked the lever, ejecting the spent cartridge, sliding a new one into the chamber, and cocking the hammer. Shouldering the weapon again, he settled his cheek against the stock, shifting his line of sight and the rifle barrel to line up the sights. He squeezed the trigger. The boy took a step backward to keep from falling as the rifle barrel jerked upward. A puff of dust burst from a stone in the well rim.

"Oh," I said with a smile. "I forgot to warn you about the kick. A rifle will jump like that when fired."

"Hurts," he said.

"You'll get used to it. Just hold the butt plate tight against your shoulder, and it will not kick so hard."

"Ain't nothin' happened to that there bottle I was shootin' at," he said with a nod toward the well.

"Your shot went low." I smiled again. "At least you hit the well. Try again."

He did not forget to work the lever this time. And his next shot pinged off the top of the rim not an inch from a bottle—I assumed it was the bottle he meant to hit. Without lowering the rifle from his shoulder, he jacked the lever and fired again, this time breaking the bottle. He did not stop to celebrate, but kept shooting, breaking the next bottle in the row, missing once, then shattering two more bottles.

The boy was a natural. He reloaded and missed but one shot, blasting every bottle on the rim and keeping his aim true after I set out another row.

The girl asked if she could try, and she handled the rifle easily and with confidence. Her shooting was not as accurate as her brother's, but she hit more often than she missed.

"Hold on," I said after she emptied the magazine. "I have something else for you to try. There is a spade in the barn. Clean up that glass while I am gone. Just throw it down the well. Watch that you do not cut yourselves."

Inside, I pawed through the pistols on the shelves until coming up with what I was looking for: a Smith and Wesson Model One-and-One-Half .32-caliber pocket revolver. I found a box of shells and rejoined the boy and girl at the well. I showed the girl how it worked.

"This is a small pistol—easy to handle for a young woman such as yourself." She blushed, but her attention did not waver. "It holds five cartridges. Unlike most revolvers, it is safe to carry fully loaded, owing to the way the hammer works." I showed her how to loosen the latch atop the back of the barrel to release the break-top and open the pistol. I handed her the cartridges, and she slipped them into the chambers.

"Them's lots littler'n what goes in that there rifle," the boy said.

"Right. The Winchester is .44 caliber. These are .32 caliber—not as powerful, but effective enough to do damage in close quarters."

The girl snapped the break-top closed. "I see the trigger. But it's tucked back in there where you can't get at it."

"It is called a 'spur trigger.' Point that pistol away from yourself and us and draw back the hammer."

"I see! It comes out when you cock the hammer."

I told her how to hold a thumb on the hammer, slowly squeeze the trigger, and lower the hammer to uncock the gun. We lined up more bottles on the rim of the well and stepped back a rod or so. "We will shoot from here. Aiming a pistol with accuracy is difficult at any distance. More so, with a small one such as this. Give it a try."

She held up the pistol with a bent elbow, and I suggested she straighten her arm.

"Them sights is mighty small. I can't hardly even see this one on the back."

"Just do your best."

The revolver popped, its burst much quieter than the rifle. The girl had jumped slightly, but the recoil was insignificant. The bullet went high, sailing off into the sagebrush. Either her aim was off, or the gun naturally shot high. In either case, she over-compensated, and the next bullet hit the rock wall. Her third shot also went astray, but she broke glass with her fourth and fifth shots. The boy tried his hand at loading and firing the pistol, and four of his five shots found their mark.

The sun had long since gone down, and the twilight was fading fast. "We had best go on inside and see what the woman has for supper. Tomorrow, there will be work to do."

Chapter Eighteen

Following a fitful night with more tossing and turning than sleep, I staggered through the curtain and into the main room, my appearance as disheveled as my mind. Four sets of eyes followed my progress across the room, intense with curiosity and, perhaps, a touch of concern—for themselves, not for me. The woman soon turned back to the stove and her cooking. The children continued to follow me with their eyes. Steaming bowls of rolled oats sweetened with molasses sat before them on the table.

"Go on with your eating," I said in a morning voice growly and grumbly. "Get that mush into you before it gets cold. Do not let it go to waste." The girl and boy went back to eating. The young girl kept watching me.

I picked a mug from the shelf, poured it full of coffee, and carried it over to the store counter. Propping myself on my elbows with both hands laced around the mug, I sipped the brew and felt its warmth radiate through my insides and its vapor clear my head. When the coffee reached the halfway point in its descent down the mug, I topped it off with a generous splash of whiskey. It was not my usual way to imbibe at first light. But something in the night had me off kilter, and I felt the need of a bracer.

The woman made a show of clanking a plate onto the table. I sat down to it and attacked the bacon and scrambled eggs with a hunger born sometime, somewhere, in the night. She put down a plate stacked with toasted bread and motioned the children to partake and followed it with a plate of bacon. The hens must not have laid eggs enough to go around. And the woman knew I did not care for boiled oats, no matter how much the molasses attempted to disguise their inherent blandness.

My disposition improved as the food and drink pushed aside the night's lingering disquiet. I took another cup of coffee, this one straight. I sipped it slowly and watched the children eat. They ate in silence, with a determination saying that if this was to be their last meal, they would make the most of it. When the bowls were scraped clean and the last of the bacon grease mopped up with the last crust of bread, I pushed back from the table.

"You two come outside with me. There is work to do."

The little girl stayed at the table and watched my every move until the door closed.

"Have you come to a decision about trading your cart for the buckboard?"

The boy and girl looked at one another, looked back at me, and the girl bowed her head.

"Is something bothering you?"

She looked back at me, her lips pressed tight. Then she said, "Ain't neither of us knows how to drive a wagon."

I laughed, which made the pair look even more uncomfortable. "What about the cart?"

The girl shook her head. "All we ever did was walk along beside the pony. If I wanted to turn or stop or somethin' I would just reach out and grab aholt of the bridle or reins or whatever come to hand."

"Well," I said, "I do not think you will have any trouble with driving." I handed the boy a halter and told him to fetch the brown mule from the big corral. I took a harness down from the barn wall. When the boy came back, I draped it over the mule and told them to get the mule harnessed and hitched. They fussed and fiddled over the job somewhat, but the cobbled together mess of a harness they used with the pony and cart had taught them the general idea, and they soon got the job done.

I tossed a pitchfork and shovel into the buckboard and stepped up and sat on the spring seat. "Come on up here, you two," I said. "See, all three of you could ride, instead of having to walk." The boy smiled at the thought, but the girl beside me was intent and watchful. The mule was well trained, and it took only a few clicks of the tongue to get him to step out. I showed the girl and boy how to hold the lines and how to pull gently on one or the other to turn the mule, and to signal a stop by drawing back on both lines, and how to put the mule into motion with a clicking tongue and fluttering of the lines. Then I handed the lines to the girl and told her to take a turn or two around the yard. Afterward, she passed them on to the boy, and I had him drive out beyond the windmill, circle around it, and do the same at the old well.

"What do you think? Think you can handle it?"

They both looked skeptical, but said they believed they could. I took the lines and drove over to the big corral, then showed them how to back up the mule, hence the wagon. "Backing takes practice. But you likely will not be called upon to do much of it, so do not worry about it. It will come to you." The rear of the wagon was at the corral gate, and I set the brake and wrapped the lines around the handle. "Climb down."

I opened the gate and handed the children the shovel and pitchfork. "Clean the muck out of the pen. Load it on the wagon, then pitch it down the old well. I will be at the house if you need me." Without waiting for a response, I went inside and fetched a mug of coffee and went out and sat on the step to soak in the day and let what was left of the night drift away on the breeze.

After a while, I watched the buckboard rattle out of the yard, the boy and girl perched upon the seat. The girl held the lines and drove the mule out to the old well and managed to get within arm's length of the hole before stopping. She and the boy stood behind the wagon and unloaded it about halfway, then climbed into the back to finish the job. Then the boy took the lines and drove back to the yard. They kept up the routine until the corral was clean. By now it was dinner time, and I walked out to the yard to call them in to eat.

I looked the corral over. Most all the manure and trampled feed was gone. "How do you feel about that mule and buckboard? Is a trade in order?"

"It don't hardly seem fair, mister," the girl said. "That there wagon and the mule is better'n what you'd get in trade."

"That is all right. As I said, I need a cart like yours around here. I will grant you that your pony is not worth much, but I will feed him up and trim his hooves and mane and tail. I believe after a time he will make a serviceable animal. So, what do you think? Deal?"

The boy grinned and fidgeted but left the talking to his sister. She swallowed hard. "I reckon if you think it's fair, we'll make the trade. But—"

I interrupted. "It is a deal, then." I extended a hand and shook with the girl and the boy to seal the bargain. "Now, unhitch your buckboard and water your mule. Then wash up and come on inside and see what the woman has fixed us for dinner."

When they came through the door, the girl said, "Mmm— somethin' sure smells good!"

The boy said, "Smells a whole lot better'n that hole out there.

Place stinks to high heaven. Smells like somethin's dead down there."

The woman had cooked up a stew of dried beef with vegetables from the root cellar. It was a lot tastier than the same dish made with desiccated vegetables. It would be a sad day when the supply the freighter brought was used up. Warm biscuits to sop up the gravy complemented the stew. But the real treat was apples the woman had baked in the oven, stuffed with raisins and seasoned with sugar and cinnamon.

"What more work we got to do to pay off that wagon and mule?" the boy said after eating.

I could see his interest came more from fatigue than a desire to work. But I had no doubt he would set his hand to any task I put before him. If not, the girl would see that he did. No matter the expression on her face, it only modified the determination that resided there.

"I had intended you would finish cleaning up the big corral," I said. "But it appears the job is done."

The boy looked relieved. The girl said, "What else is there we can do? We just as well be workin' as not." The boy gave her a look of disagreement that turned in an instant to dejection.

"When did you plan to leave us?" I said.

She shrugged. "Don't matter much. Sooner we go, sooner we'll get over to them towns and maybe find us some work."

"Well, then. Let us rest up this afternoon, then get you outfitted for the road. You can get an early start come tomorrow."

While the boy napped, the girl and her little sister watched the woman make what repairs she could to the ragged clothes the children had arrived in. I pawed through what clothes I had stored. There was not much of anything that had belonged to children, but I found a spare dress for the big girl, a jacket that would fit the boy, at least until his next growth spurt, and a small blanket the woman remade into a cape affair for the little girl.

The woman taught—as much as she could without speaking—the big girl how to handle a needle and thread. She even gave the little girl a scrap of cloth to sew on. While they worked, I put together packages of food for the children to take. Canned goods such as tomatoes and peaches that required no cooking, and jerked beef and venison. A slab of bacon. A little flour and some sugar and salt. Some loaves of bread and a sack of biscuits the woman had baked. Some raisins and rolled oats and a little jar of molasses. I even found a small bag of sweet candy drops on a shelf and tucked it into the box with the other goods. And I found a good iron skillet and a cooking pot to replace most of the salvaged cookware they came with. Those banged-up pots and pans had served mostly to carry water anyway. That job would now be taken over by a keg from my stores. It had come a long way west in its travels, but it would hold up well enough to reach the settlements to the east.

For supper, we revisited the stew and biscuits. And while we missed a repeat of the baked apples, I believe everyone to be well fed and content when we doused the lantern and went to bed. The children seemed both apprehensive and excited to meet the new day.

Morning arrived without incident. The children were already stirring when I shoved the woman out of bed and followed her through the curtain into the dim room illuminated only by the little bit of gray dawn that showed where the windows were in the dark walls. She lit a lantern, then the stove.

I struck a match and fired up another lantern and handed it to the boy. "You and your sister go on out and harness the mule and hitch up the buckboard. Give him a good drink of water first."

The little girl stayed close to the woman. They went out to

the henhouse and returned with six or eight eggs in the bucket. The woman rustled around in the bins and bags and sat the little girl at the table with a mixing bowl and spoon to stir up batter for flapjacks. The woman spooned molasses into a pan and thinned it out with water and put it on the stove to warm. She unwrapped a ham and sliced off some slabs for the skillet and tossed coffee grounds and poured water into the pot and set it to boil. Once steam rose, I poured myself a mug and carried it to the backhouse.

The wagon was at the hitchrail and the children inside eating when I came back. When we finished breakfast, there was enough light outside to see without a lamp. Not so inside. I set the lantern on the store counter and called the children over and showed them what was in the boxes the woman and I had packed. They seemed awestruck at the supplies. I suppose "not much" looked like "a whole lot" when you are accustomed to having next to nothing.

We loaded the few boxes onto the buckboard. I stowed the rifle on the floor beneath the seat. The little revolver nested in an old holster I had tacked to the sideboard within reach of the seat. I drove over to the windmill to fill the water keg and hollered out to the children to come and load up when finished. They crossed the yard, the woman with them leading the little girl by the hand. I lifted her onto the seat, and she slid to the middle. The boy and girl climbed up on either side.

I did not offer any advice. The children were resilient and had made it this far on nothing but hope. The boy and girl seemed hesitant, but that look of determination still set the girl's features. The little girl wiped away a tear as she watched the woman walk away. Then she looked at me with an altogether different expression, as if she saw something in me the others could not see. She held her gaze as the mule leaned into the harness and the buckboard rattled away across the sagebrush flat toward the slope up to the saddleback pass.

For as long as I could make out the figures on the wagon, the little girl sat cocked on the seat, watching me.

Chapter Nineteen

A few days after the children left, the man who carried the mail came over the saddleback pass. He showed up along toward evening, and as he watered his tired-out mount expressed his intention to stay the night. I told him the woman would have supper ready soon if he cared for a meal.

As we sat over drinks after eating, I asked him if he had passed anyone on the road.

"Matter of fact, I did," he said, following a sip of rye whiskey. "Damndest thing, too. It was three young'uns—all by themselves in a buckboard drawn by a brown mule."

"Children, you say?"

"Yessir. Three of 'em, like I said. A half-growed girl, maybe fifteen years old or thereabouts. A boy a few years younger, and a little girl, no more'n five, maybe six years old."

"Hmmm. That is an odd thing, I would say. You would agree, I suppose."

He mulled it over for a moment. "Seemed so to me. I talked with them a bit. They said they come over from one of them minin' towns. Folks had both died."

I said nothing, and after a moment he said, "Seems to me them kids had to've come by here."

"Yes. We saw them. They bided here a short while."

He drained off his whiskey and asked for another. "They seemed well provisioned for orphans on their own. Looked to've had plenty enough to make it to the settlements."

I nodded. "That is good."

"Funny thing, though." He sipped his whiskey. "That buckboard they was drivin'—I swear I've seen that little wagon in your yard."

"Is that right?"

"That's right. And that brown mule looked a lot like one I seen in your pens out there." He waited for a response but got none. Then, "Well?"

"Well, what?"

"How'd they come to be drivin' one of your animals pullin' one of your wagons? I don't believe they'd have the means to buy such."

I told him we had worked out a trade—they had a cart I could use, and they were in need of a wagon. Horse for mule. Simple as that.

He laughed. "Seems like a one-sided deal to me. 'Specially if what you're callin' a horse is that dirty little bangtail scrub I seen in the corral when I put my horse up. Looks like he can barely stand up but daresn't lay down for fear of not bein' able to get back up again."

"Oh, he is worn down, that is for certain. But, with some good feed and water, and a little time to rest, I suspect he will be all right."

He smiled and shook his head in disbelief. "Suppose he does? What the hell would you ever do with a scrawny little thing like that?"

I shrugged. "Same as with all the other stock that comes to hand—look for an opportunity to make a sale or trade. May well be that someone will come along needing a horse for a child."

He laughed again, louder than before. "I think what it is, is you're goin' soft. I'd of give odds bettin' against you showin' a kindness to anybody." He drained his glass and set it on the counter. "Guess I would've lost that bet."

We settled up for the meal and drinks and the water. He allowed that he would be gone in the morning and wished me a good night.

Despite his wish, the night was not a good one. I did not sleep well and, again, dreams I could not recall haunted me well into the day. I spent the morning in the yard, sorting through wagon parts that were already sorted and looking over the few oxen and horses in the pen. Next trip up to the canyon I would bring back a mule to replace the one that went with the children. As for the pony, I could not be sure he would ever recover. It may well be he would be better off dead.

After dinner, I went back out to the yard and tore down the cart taken in trade from the children. Despite my claims to the contrary, I had no need of a cart. And, had I needed a cart, it is certain this one would not serve. I was surprised it had made it this far. I knocked off the sideboards and broke down the running gear and shafts, finding no wood worthy of more than a fire. Even the iron tires on the wheels were useless, worn so thin in spots you could poke a finger through.

I was just finishing breaking the boards into kindling when yet another refugee from the mining towns drove in from the west. But here was something different.

The conveyance was a buckboard, slightly larger but not much different from the one I had traded away. The woodwork was painted a deep blue with yellow flourishes. All four wheels were new wood, unpainted. I presumed the wagon to have been recently refitted. It was drawn by a team of horses, one a good-sized bay with a blaze face and four white socks, the other a blue roan not quite as tall but on a heavier frame.

Driving the buckboard was a big brute of a man, black of skin, in workman's clothing. Beside him on the seat rode a man in business attire, right down to a buttoned vest under his suit coat, a string tie knotted at this throat, and bowler hat on his head. They drove straight to the windmill, and I met them there.

"Are you gentlemen in need of water?"

The businessman spoke. "We are, indeed. We have come far. We and the animals are in need of refreshment."

"You are welcome to drink. A dime apiece for you gentlemen. Two bits each for the horses."

The black man's eyes danced with fire, but he did not speak. The businessman served up the usual litany concerning my lack of neighborliness, the rudeness of depriving travelers of water in this desert region, and my general lack of hospitality. Nonetheless, they agreed to my price and shared the rusty cup before the driver eased the team up to the trough and allowed them to duck their muzzles into the water.

"What is on offer inside the building, and at what price?" the businessman said.

"Food and drink. I do not know what the woman is preparing for supper, but her meals are generally edible. Nothing fancy, mind you."

"And drink?"

"Coffee, of course. Bottled beer, but it is not cold. Whiskey, corn and rye. Rum."

He nodded. "I will join you for supper, and a drink afterward."

"What about him?" I said, with a nod toward the driver.

"My man will take care of himself. He prefers his own company to that of others."

I looked at the black man. "He is welcome to join us."

He said nothing, but the businessman said, "No. His duties include guarding our outfit. He prefers to keep his charge within sight."

I shrugged. "As you wish." I told the driver he could put up anywhere he chose in the yard but pointed out the fire ring. I said that there were no sleeping quarters for travelers inside, and the businessman allowed that his man would make accommodation for him at their camp, as that was their usual arrangement. He and I walked to the roadhouse.

"There is water and a towel there for washing up if you care to," I said, pointing out the washstand as we neared the door. "There is no soap." The cake I had set out for the children was back on the shelf in the store.

The woman looked our guest over when he came in. I told her he would be joining us for supper, and she turned back to her counter and started rattling pots and pans. Our guest asked for a whiskey.

"Rye or corn?"

"I believe I will try the corn. The saloons where I have been of late served only rye, and not very good rye whiskey at that. My taste for it is compromised, I fear."

I poured him a glass of the corn liquor, noting that this particular bottle came from Kentucky. He sipped it and nodded his approval.

"Where is it you have been 'of late,' if you do not mind my asking."

He shook his head. "Not at all. Not at all. I have been in the vicinity of the mines in the mountains. Banking is my trade, and I had banks in two communities there. Alas, with the take from the mines diminished to almost nothing, there is little need for my services in the towns, and little profit in it for me. So, I decided to liquidate my holdings there and relocate to environs with better prospects."

"And where might that be? If you do not mind my asking."

"Not at all." He emptied his glass and held it up to signal a refill. I poured a generous amount, and he swallowed a good portion of it in one drink. "Once we reach the city, I will board an eastbound train and return to my family and partners. My father is engaged in banking and finance in Boston. I will consult with Father—as well as my uncles and brothers—as to my next venture. Perhaps I will stay in Boston." He shrugged and emptied his drink and again signaled for another.

A few drinks later, the aromas from the woman's cooking permeated the air, and the banker said he was looking forward to a home-cooked meal.

"Your driver is welcome to eat with us. It could be he, too, would welcome a break from camp cooking."

"Thank you, no. As I said, he would rather keep to himself." He finished yet another drink and, as had been the case for the last few, refilled the glass himself. "And, I prefer that he keep an eye on my belongings." He winked at me and drained his glass.

He kept the glass at hand as he partook of the meal of fried ham, beans and bacon sweetened with molasses, warm cornbread, cheese, and sour pickles. We returned to the store counter—or bar, in its present use—and I set out another bottle of the Kentucky whiskey. I drank coffee, and he drank whiskey. The banker had, by then, imbibed a goodly amount of the stuff, but he showed no ill effects. He seemed as steady as ever.

Perhaps he felt the effects of the whiskey despite appearances, for after a few minutes he said he wanted to sit. I carried the lantern over to the table, and he followed with his glass. He sat, took a drink, and looked at the glass. "Damnation! I forgot the bottle."

"Are you sure you need more? You have had a lot of it."

"Not enough. Not yet." He started to get up.

"Sit down. I will get it." But, instead of retrieving the bottle, I reached under the counter and grabbed a short length of cord. As I approached the table, I raised and crossed my arms, dropped the cord over his head, then uncrossed my arms and pulled the cord tight, cutting off his yell and his wind. He tried to stand, but I held him in the chair. He scratched and clawed at the cord, but it was too tight to allow any purchase. He stomped and kicked, but all he managed to do was drum on the floor and slide the table away with his thrashing. Finally, he sagged into stillness. I kept the pressure on the cord, even pulled it tighter.

I undressed the banker down to his underwear where he sat, leaving his clothes in a heap under the table, and left him sitting. I carried the lantern back to the counter and found the heavy Colt's revolver I kept under there with the loaded shotgun. I checked the cylinder and slipped a cartridge into the empty hole.

Leaving the lantern where it sat, I walked out into the darkness. I went slowly, as if I was unsure of the way and a bit unsteady on my feet. As I rounded the corner of the roadhouse, I could see the driver, his back to me, silhouetted against his fire. He heard me coming and turned to look. He could not make me out in the darkness, of course, and assumed—as I hoped he would—that I was the banker coming to bed.

He did not look again until I was two or three yards away and, as he turned, the side of his head disintegrated under the force of the heavy bullet that ripped its way into and through his skull, all but tearing the top of his head off as it blew out the opposite side, the blood spatter hissing in the flames of the campfire.

I threw more wood onto the fire to create more light. The driver had put the horses in the small pen attached to the barn, and I led them out and put the harnesses on and hitched them to the wagon. It took enough effort to work up a sweat undressing the driver and getting him onto the buckboard. I drove around the roadhouse, went inside, and slung the banker over my shoulder, carrying him out and dumping him onto the wagon beside his driver, returning for his clothing.

Down the old well both bodies went.

Most of what they carried was still on the buckboard. I

stopped beside the fire and tossed what camp equipment the driver had unloaded, along with his clothes, onto the wagon and parked it in the barn bay and closed the doors. I dared not keep the horses at the place for fear they would attract unwanted attention, so I put them on a lead, saddled the old mare, and set out in the night for the canyon.

Metallic smell. Coppery. The smell of blood. Stabbing head pain. Eyes veiled behind lashes, looking for realization slow to come.

The boy raises himself on his elbows, and chaotic images unwind and attack memory. Raised hands, bended knees, met by bayonet and buttstock, bullet and blade. Lifeblood from soldiers black and white, melding red and red on the ground. Gunboat ports blind. Rolling fire of rifles. Arrowpoint of death escaping down the bluff toward the river. Man-on-man ladders scaling futile parapets. Whistle and whiz and hiss and whisper of sharpshooter shots.

The boy pushes aside a body fallen across his legs and rises. Swipes sticky, wet scalp with shirtsleeve. Blue tunics, with fallen soldiers inside, strewn about. In places, so thick and deep they must be trod upon. The boy turns and wheels and stumbles, unsure in which direction salvation lies. Secessionist soldiers follow their own long shadows, abandoning the field. Bloodstained survivors wade through the carnage, seeking life.

The boy slumps to the bloody mud and sobs.

CHAPTER TWENTY

The sun was well up when I left the canyon and set out for home. A few miles down the trail, I watched a cloud of dust coming my way. When the horsemen drew near, I reined up and waited. The lieutenant leading the cavalry patrol looked so young as to still be a stranger to the straight razor. His skin was unweathered and his uniform unfaded, and I assumed his assignment to the fort to be his first. He ordered a halt, military school parade ground style, and the grizzled sergeant riding behind raised a hand with a bemused look on his face. The troopers, likewise, smiled at the spit and polish of their leader.

"State your business," the officer said.

I could not help but smile at his officiousness. "Hello yourself. And a good morning to you."

"I asked you a question, mister. I expect an answer."

Smile still intact, I pulled my right foot out of the stirrup and swung the leg over the old mare's neck, and relaxed into a slouch as limp as the lieutenant's posture was stiff. "The truth is, you did not ask a question at all, officer. You as much as ordered me to state my business. But, as you see, I am not wearing a uniform and am not obligated to respond to commands from a shavetail lieutenant such as yourself."

Snickering and suppressed laughter among the troopers drew a quick rebuke.

I smiled and nodded at the sergeant. While you could not say we were acquainted, I had seen him before, on similar patrols.

Given their direction of travel, I was fairly certain the soldiers had ridden out of the fort and traveled through the reservation to see what the Paiutes were up to, met the old stage road, then left it for the trail up the long valley and back to the fort. More than likely they had bivouacked somewhere along the way, set out early, and stopped at my place for water.

"Sergeant."

He returned the nod. "How's things?"

I said things were about as expected.

"Saw your woman. Stopped for water down at your place this morning."

"I am on my way back there now."

"What you been up to?"

I pointed at the rifle in the scabbard tied to the saddle. "Out hunting for some deer meat for the kettle."

"Looks like you ain't had much luck."

"Looks like. They are about, but I did not see anything worth wasting a bullet on."

"Maybe next time."

I nodded. "Maybe next time." The old mare stood quiet, but the cavalry horses pawed and snorted and shook their heads, rattling bit chains and headstalls. "Tell that quartermaster sergeant at the fort that I have come by a few horses of late, should he be looking for remounts. I have one or two that would make fine mounts for your commander—top quality stock. Showy."

The sergeant smiled. "Spoken like a true horse trader."

I shrugged.

"I'll tell him." The sergeant arched his back, then squirmed his way into a more comfortable seat in the saddle. "Lieutenant, we had best be on the trail."

The young officer scowled, as if reminding the sergeant who gave the orders. He snapped out a string of the same kind of military school parade ground commands as before. Most of the troopers smiled, and, when the sergeant waved his hand forward, they moved out in a disorderly fashion that likely set the lieutenant's teeth on edge.

Back home, I put up the mare and went inside to see what I could find in the way of food. It had been a long night and morning since my last meal. I had no sooner closed the door than the woman put a plate of fried eggs and ham and yesterday's beans and cornbread on the table. By the time I sat down, there was a mug full of coffee steaming beside the plate.

I did away with the meal in short order, and the woman poured more coffee. "Anybody come by on the road?"

She shook her head. I picked up the empty plate and sailed it at her. It hit the arm holding the coffeepot and the liquid splashed her dress, the hot fabric clinging to her skin and blistering her arm and thigh. The woman trembled, and her breath hissed between clenched teeth, but she did not move from where she stood.

"Funny thing. Soldiers I talked to a while ago said they saw you. I guess you did not notice them." Her eyes burned as dark and hot as the spilled coffee. I pushed back from the table. "Clean up that mess."

Out in the yard, I propped the barn door partway open to let in some light. I set aside the clothing from the banker and his bodyguard and sorted through what was on the wagon. There was the usual selection of camp equipment, most of it in better condition than I typically found. It would make a nice addition to my stores. There was a trunk filled with the banker's clothing—another business suit that would be unlikely to find a buyer, but also some little-used everyday clothing I suspect he wore when going out to inspect his investments. I cast aside a pair of polished shoes of soft leather with thin soles, not seeing any prospect of needing such for a fancy ball or visit to a high-toned theater.

Shoved against the back of the spring seat, buried under a rolled-up canvas tent and a gunnysack of oats for the team, was a smallish trunk reinforced with metal all around, secured with a padlock. I slid it to the back of the wagon, climbed down and let it drop to the ground. Its weight told me I had found what I expected to find. With the blunt side of an ax, I broke loose the hasp and staple, and the lock fell off.

Inside were several small leather pouches filled with gold dust and nuggets. Under the bags was a double stack of banded bank notes. I riffled through a few of the bundles but did not bother to count the money. Beneath the currency, covering the bottom of the box, were several gold ingots and rows of gold coins. Apparently, business had been good at the banks before the mines played out. Back into the box went my newfound wealth. I wrapped a leather belt the bodyguard had worn around the box to secure the lid and cached it near where I had stowed the bank robber's loot.

It was time to give some serious thought to relocating to a more civilized place where I could live out my days in comfort and leisure. But, for now, there was work to do.

I broke off and broke up the wagon box and burned it, the fancy-paint job too recognizable to keep. I pushed the running gear out into the yard and parked it where the little buckboard had been. I pulled off the wheels and leaned them against the wall of a shed where sun and wind would scour a little more of the newness off them. Finally, I removed the tongue from the running gear and replaced it with shafts by way of further disguise.

Then I went inside. Supper should be ready soon. And I could use some more coffee.

For several days we saw no traffic on the road save the mail carrier on his way back to the settlements. He rode around the old well a time or two, studying the ground and looking down the hole in an attempt to find something there, but did not. At the windmill, he cast his eyes over the yard, taking it all in. When his horse finished watering, he came inside for a meal.

When the woman refilled his coffee mug, he grabbed her wrist and held her arm still. He slid the sleeve up a few inches to reveal more of the burn marks from the spilled coffee. The blisters were gone, but the flesh was still red and raw.

"That's a pretty serious burn you got there, ma'am. What happened?"

She stared at him for a moment, her look revealing nothing, then pulled her hand away and went back to the stove. After leaving the coffeepot there to warn, she made her way to the bedroom and pushed through the curtain.

"What happened?"

I shrugged. "Spilled some coffee is all. She will heal. It may teach her not to be so clumsy."

He gave me a half nod and sat sipping his coffee for a while. Then, "That old well out there . . ."

I let the silence stand for a time. "You do seem to take an unhealthy interest in it. What is it that is troubling you?"

"The stink comin' up out of that hole could curl a man's hair." He locked his eyes on mine and cut a furrow between his eyebrows.

"You recall those children that came through here a while back? The ones I traded that little buckboard to?"

Again, the half nod.

"Well, the two older ones took on some work to help pay for the provisions I sold them. Had them clean the manure and muck out of the big corral and pitch it down the well. I suspect that stuff is getting pretty ripe down there. The smell will fade after a while—leastways it always has."

He did not look convinced. He wagged his head slowly back and forth. "Smells more like somethin' dead."

I shrugged and let his opinion lie.

"Speakin' of that little buckboard, I see where you've replaced it already—there's another wagon out there where it was—leastways the guts of one."

"You have a sharp eye. Not to mention more curiosity than a man ought to have where it is none of his affair. But since you asked, more or less, I have had that running gear for some time—parked in one of the sheds. I decided I would get it outfitted with a box, put a seat on it, maybe a coat of paint." I paused for a taste of coffee. "Kind of lost interest in it. But I will get to it in my own good time."

The man who carried the mail finished his coffee, said he wanted to put some miles behind him before dark, and rode away. I sat on the step with my coffee and watched him cross the sagebrush flat, ride up the slant to the saddleback pass, and disappear into the day. Tossing away the dregs of my coffee, I walked out to the old well.

The man was right. It smelled like death.

A day or two later the freighter came through. I watched him ride past the windmill. He saw me watching, smiled his little smile, and tipped his silly hat with a flourish. But he stopped when I hailed him.

I stood looking up at him on his seat on the Murphy wagon. "I am surprised to see you again."

He removed his hat and mopped the sweat band with a handkerchief, then used it to mop the top of his head. "I confess I'm some surprised m'self. But, I got a wire sayin' they had the better part of a load to be hauled. Ordered up some supplies, too, they did—not anywhere near a wagon load, but it's better'n deadheading."

"I wish I had known you were coming. I could use some more of those root vegetables."

"Too bad there ain't no telegraph here." He looked around the valley, empty save for his immediate surroundings. "Don't guess there ever will be, anymore."

"How is that lame ox of yours? Did he make it home all right?"

"Oh, yes. Didn't take no hurt. Put him on my other wagon. The roads it travels is a hell of lot better'n this'n. Rough as a cob, this'n, in places. Man's got to be careful not to bust a wheel or snap an axle—or lame up an ox." He wiped the back of his neck, then his forehead with the limp handkerchief, and stuffed it down the bib of his overalls. "Reckon I had best be gettin' on."

"Got enough water?"

He smiled. "Likely not quite as much in them kegs as these oxen'll need 'fore we reach the next water—but, at the prices you charge, we'll get by."

The wagon creaked into motion and I watched it move away, framed against a sky yellowed by the low-hanging sun. The freighter had not traveled a mile when a horseman coming the opposite direction passed him coming my way. I watched him come and after a bit saw the rider lean out and spit a long stream of tobacco juice. I hurried into the roadhouse and fetched the shotgun from beneath the counter. It was the drover from Arkansas, who paid to water his herd here under threat of violence.

He reined up a few yards from where I stood in the road. He spat another stream of syrupy tobacco juice. "You are mighty fond of that scattergun, mister. Seems like it goes everywhere you do."

"As I recall, we did not part on the best of terms. I was—am—unsure of your intentions."

"Just passin'."

"I also recall you said in no uncertain terms that you would not be coming this way again."

"Well, here's the deal. I figured I could afford a drink of water for me and my horse, since it's just the two of us. 'Course when I bring the families and more stock out to California, I will take the trail up north. But I am in a hurry to get back to Arkansas 'fore the weather turns, and this road is shorter." He spat again.

"Go ahead and water your horse, gratis—just so you know there are no hard feelings."

Wrinkles radiated out from his smile. "Why, that's mighty big of you." He spat. "Not that you've got any reason to be harborin' ill will towards me."

He dismounted and led the horse to the trough.

"How did you find California? Was it all you hoped for?"

The drover leaned against the windmill tower, spat the wad from his cheek onto the ground, then fingered a plug of tobacco from one vest pocket, a jackknife from the other, and whittled off another cud. He worked it around until moist, tucked it into his cheek with his tongue, and spat. "Found it right hospitable. Got there with every cow we left Arkansas with—save ten head we got snookered out of by you. Place is a whole hell of a lot different from back home. Not so much rain. Not so many trees. But grass—damn! I swear if a feller was to set real still, he could hear it growin'."

He chewed and spat some more. "We sold what steers we had left for a good price. The cows all look to be carryin' calves, so the herd'll grow. I'll be puttin' together a bigger herd to bring out with the women and young'uns. Have to hire some help to herd 'em—the cattle, that is—but there ain't no shortage of men lookin' for a ticket to California."

He spat again. "As you can see, mister, I'm travelin' light.

Could I trouble you for supper?"

"Of course. Fifty cents for the meal. All the water and coffee you care to drink to go with it."

"Fifty cents, you say. I swear, mister, there ain't a way to skin a traveler that you ain't thought of. Fifty cents!" He emphasized his displeasure with another stream of tobacco juice.

"Put your horse in the big corral with the other stock. You'll see a washstand hanging on the wall by the roadhouse door. Plenty of water and a towel to dry off with, but there is no soap."

CHAPTER TWENTY-ONE

When I heard the drover splashing at the washstand, I told the woman to dish up the supper. I heard him toss the water he washed with from the basin and pour in more. The man must be particular about cleanliness. He came in and I told him to have a seat. The plates sat on the table wisping steam.

I was standing at the store counter lighting a lamp, as it had grown dim in the room. I watched the drover sit. The woman stepped over from the stove and put a mug of coffee in front of him, and another at my place. The drover looked at the woman, looked down at his supper plate, and back at the woman.

He pushed back from the table, never taking his eyes from the woman. "Pardon me." He walked over to the counter. "You expect me to eat that stuff?"

I drew back and studied his face. "Is there something wrong with the food? You did not even taste it."

"That woman—she's Indian, ain't she."

"Yes. Paiute, as it happens."

"You expect me to eat somethin' cooked by a dirty Indian?"

I stared at the man.

"That woman—she your wife?"

I nodded. "I suppose so. Common law."

He shook his head. "Ain't no accountin' for a man like you. You may as well take up with a darky as a dirty Indian."

I could only stare.

"Indians ain't no better'n animals. Man may as well have

relations with a sheep, or a milk cow."

My eyes were riveted to his face as I picked up the shotgun lying there on the counter where I had left it to light the lantern. The drover took a step back and put his hand atop the butt of the holstered revolver at his waist.

"You had best move your hand away from that pistol, slowly. If you so much as attempt to draw it, I will blow your head off." I pulled back the hammers on both barrels. His eyes flinched as the hammers ratcheted into position, and he lifted his hand from the gun, then raised the other, both palms facing me.

"I—"

"Shut your mouth. There is nothing to be said." I motioned with the shotgun. "Turn around." He did, and I stepped up behind him and lifted his revolver and slid it into my waistband. "Now, get the hell out of my house. And do not try anything. I am right behind you." I poked him with the shotgun barrel to get him moving.

Outside, I walked him over to the old well. "Turn around."

He turned to face me. His eyes looked both worried and defiant. He worked his jaw as if his mouth were dry. "Mind if I take some tobacco?"

I shook my head. "You will not have time to taste it." I prodded him with the shotgun, walking him backward until stopped by the rock rim.

His forehead creased and eyes squinted in a look of pure hatred. "I suppose you're goin' to shoot me now, you Indian-lovin' sonofabitch."

"You are not worth the powder."

I did not shoot him. Instead, I shoved the shotgun barrel hard into his chest. He shuffled his feet, trying to keep his balance, but I kept pushing until he fell backward over the wall.

He screamed going down, but his voice stopped suddenly when his head hit the side of the well. The rest of him stopped just as suddenly a few seconds later when he hit the bottom.

I went back inside for supper. I still had some appetite left after finishing my plate, so I ate what was on his as well. Then I treated myself to a glass of rum. And then another.

Come the morning, feeling fresh after a rare night of restful sleep, I did my business in the backhouse, then set out to deal with what the drover left behind.

His saddle stood on its fork with the saddle blanket draped over it, hair-side up, to dry. An old Henry rifle in a saddle scabbard, and a long narrow bag lay beside it. I sat on his spread-out bedroll and untied the bag and dumped out a small sack of flour, even smaller sacks of salt and sugar, a sack of beans, a slab of bacon wrapped in greasy cloth, a bundle of jerky, a sack of coffee inside a camp-size pot, a small frying pan, and another small, but deeper, pan.

I looked around for someplace else he might have stored his valuables. I pulled the saddle blanket off the saddle, but it revealed no saddlebags. I found them under the bedroll. Whether he put them there for a pillow or to hide them, I neither knew nor cared. The saddlebag flaps were secured with leather ties. Inside the one was a shirt rolled around a pair of socks and long underwear. A bag of tools and other trappings for minor repairs filled the rest of the bag—a knife in a sheath, an awl, a spool of heavy thread and a needle, a bundle of whang leather, some rolled-up sheets of tanned leather and rawhide, a hoof pick, and some horseshoe nails and a small hammer.

I sat looking at the pile, cussing myself for not emptying the drover's pockets. I would never know what he had secreted on his person. I hoped it was not the sum total of his wealth as I opened the opposite saddlebag. Out came a box of .44-caliber rimfire cartridges that would fit both the rifle in the scabbard and his revolver, still tucked into my waistband.

The only other thing in the saddlebag was a rolled-up cloth

bag. I tested its weight as I pulled it out, and the heft indicated something substantial inside. I rolled it out, picked up the bottom, and dumped it out onto the bedroll. It was what I was looking for.

Not as much as I hoped for, mind you. But there was a bundle of paper money and a pouch with a handful of gold eagles.

The drover was right. He got a pretty good price for his steers in California. I had a fleeting hope that his cow herd would produce many more over the years, providing well for his family.

It was quiet for the next week or so. Then one day a wagon came over the saddleback pass. As it crossed the sagebrush flat toward me it struck me as an odd arrangement. The wagon was drawn by a team of oxen, which was not unusual. But two other oxen were trailing the wagon on leads. Some travelers, those with the means, sometimes carried a spare ox, but I could not remember ever having seen a spare team. Also, walking along beside the wagon were two men, one with a whip, the handle of which served as a goad, two women, one with a small child in her arms, and six other children ranging from half-grown to a couple small enough that they had to break into a run from time to time to keep up. Sitting on the wagon seat was an old lady with a child on her lap.

I walked out to the windmill to meet them. "Good afternoon."

The man with the whip nodded a greeting. "And to you." He looked behind me to the trough. "That looks like sweet water there. We are in need of refreshment."

I looked at the motley assortment of humankind. "Two bits apiece for the animals."

Both men looked surprised. The old lady on the wagon snorted. "Two bits! Why, that's inhuman of you to put such a price on God's bounty." She set her jaw and her lips cut a narrow gash in a face now red.

"Ma, hold your peace," the whip man said, all the while keeping his eyes on me. "But she does have a point."

"The water is God's bounty. With that I would not disagree. However, God was content to leave it in the ground. It is my windmill that brings it to the surface. And that comes at a price." I again looked them over. "My customary charge for people is ten cents apiece—"

I got no further before the old lady interrupted me with another tirade about my lack of humanity and so on. I let her finish as the rest of the company shifted back and forth, traced lines in the dust with their toes, studied their fingernails, and the like. When she finished, I told them what I had intended to tell them in the first place—that if they would pay the dollar for the four oxen, they were all free to drink their fill.

One of the women filled and refilled the rusty tin cup from the pipe and handed it in turn to the others, children first, then the adults. When all had a drink, she started again, offering more to all who wanted it, and most did.

"If you do not mind my saying so, you have a lot more people than I have ever seen with one wagon."

"It ain't by choice, that's for damn sure."

"Then what?"

He looked me over for a minute and handed the whip to the other man. "Mind if we set down?"

"Come on over to the yard. We will find some shade." We sat with our backs against the roadhouse wall in the narrow strip of its shadow.

"Three nights ago, we was camped by a little spring—last water we seen 'fore gettin' to here. Wind come up in the night whilst we was sleepin'. Near as we could figure, it must've blowed some embers from the cookfire onto the cover of our other wagon—the one belongin' to my brother—and set it afire."

He swallowed hard and scrubbed his face with the palms of his hands. "Whole thing was blazin' 'fore we woke up. Weren't a thing we could do about it. Tried to douse it with water from the spring, but we never had but the one bucket, and the way the wind was whippin' them flames . . ."

"Was anyone hurt?"

He shook his head. "Not really—my brother, he burnt his hands some tryin' to get stuff off the wagon." He shook his head again. "But it weren't no use. Lost it all but a bit of food and the kitchen box we'd unloaded so's the women could do the cookin'. That, and our blanket rolls. Most all the rest burnt up so bad we couldn't keep it."

"What all did you lose?"

"Well, here's the thing. Since we're travelin' together to get to California, we never kept our goods apart—you know, my family's things in my wagon, my brother's in his. Instead, we loaded farmin' tools and implements, and what furniture we took, in my wagon. In his, we carried our bedding, foodstuff, clothes, and some of the household stuff." He stopped and wiped his eyes with a crumpled rag from his pocket. "What was left from his wagon, we loaded on mine—stuff to make camp, and whatnot—and now it's loaded so heavy the team can't hardly pull it."

"You have the other team. Why not double up?"

He shook his head. "We ain't got but the one yoke. His was settin' on the back end of the tongue ag'in the wagon box. Yoke got burnt pretty bad, and the bows burnt right through. We trade off the teams to spell 'em, but, still, it's slow goin' with such a heavy load."

"What about your food provisions?"

He threw up his hands then let them fall back into his lap. "What little bit we could save is 'bout gone. Don't know where we'll restock."

We sat without talking for a few minutes. He watched the families. The children, refreshed by the water, laughed and played around the wagon.

"I hope you won't think unkindly of Ma for what she said. She ain't normally inclined to rude behavior. I reckon all the troubles has got her upset."

He said they had come from Indiana. The brothers worked the family farm, which had provided a good living for their late father's family, but with both their growing families relying on it, they found themselves stretched thin. So, they had decided to sell out and try their luck in California.

Like most of the travelers on this road, they had wanted to save time and miles by coming this way, rather than following the main trail up north. And, like most travelers on this road, they found it more difficult than anticipated, given the distances between reliable water, the lack of settlements where they could resupply, and the dearth of assistance should illness or accident befall them.

Nor were they aware that some who travel this road simply disappear without a trace.

CHAPTER TWENTY-TWO

After listening to his tale of woe, I invited the Indiana farmer to set up camp in the yard. I told him I carried supplies and had on hand most of what he needed, from food staples to a wagon to replace the one that burned. I asked if he could pay.

He looked at me for a time before answering. "We have money. Some. But what we got is meant to get us set up in California." He paused again. "It pains me to say it, but if your prices is anything like what you ask for a drink of water, well, I don't reckon we can afford to pay 'em."

I did not answer right away. I watched the children playing a game of tag, running around the wagon and windmill and trough chasing after one another. "Go ahead and set up camp and get settled in. I believe we can come to terms."

We stood and brushed the dust off the seats of our pants. I asked if they had enough food for their dinner.

"We'll get by."

"Well, do not go hungry. And make sure the children get fed. There will be time after dinner to see to what you need."

I went inside, and the woman spooned me up a bowl of beans and some biscuits saved over from breakfast. As I sat down, I told her to fix up as big a batch of soup or stew as she could so we could provide supper for the Indiana farmers. But she was already peeling potatoes and cutting up carrots and turnips from piles on the countertop. Apparently, she had taken stock of our visitors and paid a visit to the root cellar. I wondered how much her generosity had depleted our stock of vegetables.

After a cup of coffee, I walked between the store shelves and gathered an assortment of clothing and stacked it in piles on the table. I hefted bags of beans and flour and rice out in front of the counter. Atop the counter went a bag of coffee beans, a sack of sugar, a bag of salt, some corn meal, rolled oats, and other assorted goods. The woman brought over a ham and some slabs of bacon.

By that time, I figured the farmers would be finished with the midday meal and walked out and around the roadhouse to the yard. The two brothers were already looking over the wagons and running gear and wagon parts. I knew either of the two wagons there would serve their purpose. Or, we could assemble one from the running gear, boxes, and bows on hand.

They saw me coming, and as I walked up, the farmer I had talked to earlier said, "You've a goodly amount of equipment. How'd you come by it all, way out here?"

I looked from him to his brother and back again. "Most all of it was taken in trade. Got the rest of it one way or another. Tore down a lot of broken-down wagons for parts." I shrugged. "I sell something from time to time. Folks get out this far and find their wagons in need of repair or parts. I can replace most anything on a wagon."

The farmers had their eye on one particular wagon. They crawled under it to inspect the condition of the reach and hounds, axles and bolsters. They checked every clip, every bolt, every washer, every rod, every bracket, every rivet, every staple to ensure they were tight and showing no more than an acceptable amount of wear. They wandered through the spare tongues and axles and wheels and boxes, looking for possibilities of improvement. I brought out canvas covers from a shed where I stored them out of the weather. They unfolded and examined every one, setting aside those with rips and tears, inspecting the repairs on others, and finally choosing what they considered to be the best of them. They looked over the three yokes on hand, tested the bows and keys for fit, and made their choice.

If nothing else, these Indiana farmers were meticulous. I watched it all from a few steps behind them so as not to overhear their whispered discussions. The older brother, who seemed to speak for the families, brushed the dust from his hands, then wiped them on his pants legs.

He nodded toward their choice of wagon. "This one here looks like it would do the job."

I waited, saying nothing.

"Do you suppose . . ." he said, then paused for moment. "Do you suppose we could trade out the wheels for them over there?" He pointed to the relatively new set of wheels on the running gear from the banker's buckboard. "Those ones look to be in better shape. They be the same size, so the skeins on these axles ought to fit those boxes just fine."

Kneading my chin with one hand, I looked from the wagon to the running gear, back and forth, back and forth. "Is there something wrong with the wheels on that wagon?"

He shook his head. "Not much. The felloes on the right rear wheel shows some gaps, and a few of the spokes has some play in 'em. Likely just shrunk up from dryness." He waited while I thought that over. Then, "It's mostly just that them other wheels is in better shape. Less likely to break down—not that them on the wagon would, but, well, you know—it just makes more sense to get the best, if you can."

I said nothing but went into the same shed as before and carried out a wagon jack and wheel wrench. I dropped them at the farmer's feet. "You swap them out. And make certain the wheels you put on that running gear are properly installed." I had no doubt they would be. "First, we should talk money."

The farmer hemmed and hawed and eventually said they

189

could not come up with a price.

"Well," I said, "prices out here are likely a good deal higher than what a wagon like that would bring in more settled places. If you do not like my price, you could not go down the street to another wagon yard or to the next town and make a better deal. About the only choice you face is to take it, or leave it."

He nodded. "That is true."

I let them stew for a few minutes, pursing my lips, wrinkling my brow, scratching my head, and otherwise giving the impression of serious thought and calculation. Then, "What did your wagons set you back in Indiana?"

The farmer told me the wagon that burnt up had been one of their farm wagons. And he told me the price of the other wagon, purchased from a neighboring farmer. "On top of that, we spent some money puttin' on bows and covers, water barrels, and such like."

After a further period of consideration, during which I walked around the wagon, looking it over, I told the brothers I could let this one go at the same price they had paid in Indiana—but only because they were in a fix, and I did not see any need to inconvenience or impoverish them. I said the stated price would cover my expenses, but only just.

The Indiana farmers were surprised nearly to the point of looking shocked. Then they tried not to smile, but without much luck. We shook hands all around, then the men went to work swapping wheels. While they worked, I invited the two wives and the old lady into the house to see what we had on hand in the way of food supplies. I gave them an estimate of the days it would take to make it to the mining towns where they might pick up some supplies, and how much longer it should take to reach California.

The women were as meticulous as their men. One held a baby, and the other had a little child barely able to walk in hand. They shook out and held up piece after piece of clothing, eyeing it for fit. There was not much available in the way of clothing for children, but they found a few garments that would help resupply the wardrobes. They had better luck with dresses. Nothing fancy, mind you, but trail clothes of sturdy fabric. Likewise, a spare shirt each that would fit the men. The wives seemed pleased with what they found, but the old lady "tsk-tsked" over mended rips and tears, stains and smudges. The wives assured her the clothing was fine—better than what they wore, in some instances, and certainly superior to nothing, which—owing to the misfortune of the fire—was all they owned, beyond what they wore.

All the while, the pleasing smells of the stew simmering on the stove filled the air. The wives commented on it occasionally, and one time the old lady went to the stove and lifted the lid from the pot, inhaling deeply the aromas rising with the steam. She went so far as to pick up the spoon and give the stew a stir, studying the contents.

They set aside the chosen clothing. I asked about shoes. The wives claimed all the children had adequate shoes, save the oldest girl. She was growing so fast, they said, that her shoes were painfully tight, even though they had a lot of wear left in them. Her feet, in fact, almost filled her mother's shoes. We found a well-worn but adequate pair and added them to the pile.

The old lady sat at the table, and I poured her some coffee. The wives looked at the food supplies I had set out, and I invited them to look through the shelves for other stock. They joined the old lady at the table, and I poured them coffee. They sipped and talked, listing what and how much they might need in the way of food to stock the wagon.

While they talked, the woman came through the curtain. She stopped and looked them over; they eyed her with equal intensity. The woman came to the stove and checked her stew.

One of the wives cleared her throat. "Good afternoon, ma'am."

The woman said nothing, keeping to her work and rattling pans as she set them on the counter.

"I must say, that is a lovely ragout you have prepared," the old lady said.

The woman turned and looked at her with a wrinkled brow, unsure of what she had heard.

"I'm sorry. I suppose 'stew' is the more common way of sayin' it. My mama came over from France, and her way of talkin' sticks with me, sometimes."

The woman nodded.

"I see you are fixin' to prepare something. Can we be of help?"

The woman said nothing.

I said, "She does not talk."

"You mean she does not talk English?"

"No. I mean she does not speak at all."

All three of the Indiana women watched me, waiting to see what I would say next. I cleared my throat and swallowed hard. "She does not have a tongue."

Again, they waited.

"It was cut out, long ago."

The women exchanged glances, looked at the Paiute woman, and at me. They all looked as if they wanted to say something but could not find the words.

When the silence grew uncomfortable, I said that the stew was intended for their families. That started another round of exchanged looks.

The woman turned back to her work shuffling pans and dumped some flour into a big bowl.

The old lady stood and walked over to stand beside her. She looked over the ingredients the woman had laid out. "I see you are makin' biscuits."

The woman looked sidewise at her and nodded.

"Let me help." Without waiting for an answer, the old lady took over the work.

Stepping back, the woman watched her until satisfied the old lady knew her way around a batch of biscuits. Then she fetched more bowls, put them on the table, and set out ingredients for some other concoction.

A dollop of fat and some sugar went into the biggest bowl, and the Indiana wives watched as she stirred and mixed them. The woman cracked in some eggs.

"Oh, my!" one of the wives said. "I can't recall when last I seen a fresh egg."

The woman stirred a while longer, then spooned in a lot of molasses. From another bowl, she dumped in some flour mixed with a little salt and some cinnamon and some other spice, then kept stirring and pouring in water until it stirred to her satisfaction. Then she rubbed fat all over the inside of a squarish pan and poured in the mixture. I had no idea what it was or what it might become.

By that time, the old lady had the biscuits rolled out and cut and in the pan. The woman slid the biscuits and the other pan into the oven and fiddled with the knobs and levers on the stove. No sooner had she shut the door than she started another batch of biscuits, and no sooner had she started than the old lady stepped in and again took over the work. The woman smiled a little and stood aside. The wives gathered up the bowls and other tools the women had used and set to washing them out in the tub at the end of the counter.

By then I had seen enough of women's work for one day. Besides, the smell of the simmering stew, baking biscuits, and whatever else the woman had in the oven was making my mouth water. I stepped outside and went around to the yard to see how the men were coming with the wagon. The farmers were apparently as efficient as they were meticulous. The new wheels were on the wagon, and they were lashing down the cover over the bows. I could see the old wheels were already on the running gear, as well.

I had no idea what all the children had been up to. I looked around and saw some of them playing around in the barn. Some of the smaller ones were at the campsite, sitting on a blanket with some little toys of some sort. I caught a movement out of the corner of my eye and looked to see a little boy over by the old well. He walked around and around the rock rim, tapping it with a stick. He stopped, stood on his toes, leaned over the edge, and dropped the stick down the hole.

"Hey!"

The boy did not hear me. He scraped up a handful of rocks and pebbles, raised himself on his toes again, leaned over the well shaft and tossed the stones in one at a time.

"Hey!" I said again as I hurried over to the well. Then I thought not to yell again, as I might startle the boy. He gathered more pebbles, and this time stuck the toes of his shoes in the indentations in the rock wall, trying to climb. He was maybe a foot off the ground and leaning well over the edge when I reached him. I did not say anything but wrapped an arm around the boy and pulled him back.

He turned and looked at me, let out a holler, and started kicking and screaming. I held tight to him and backed away from the well. By then his father, the younger of the men, was running to us. He grabbed the boy from my arms, held him up and gave him a shake, then set him firmly on the ground. The boy was shaking and sniffling, with tears making tracks down his dusty cheeks.

I squatted down in front of the boy and took his hands in mine. "That old well is deep. If you were to fall in, we could never get you out. You would spend eternity down there. And, boy, with all the trash we throw down that hole, it would not be a pleasant place to be. You would not notice it, of course, being dead from the fall."

The boy stopped sniffling. He pulled one of his hands away and used the back of it for a handkerchief, wiping his nose. With both hands, he scoured the tears from his eyes.

I stood up, looked at the father, and shook my head. "I am sorry. I did not mean to scare him."

"That's fine. You likely saved the boy's life. I'd trade that for a few tears anytime."

He took the boy by the hand, and we started back to the yard. We had not gotten far when one of the wives stepped around the corner of the roadhouse and called us in to supper.

CHAPTER TWENTY-THREE

Never had so many people been in the roadhouse at one time. Perhaps, maybe, back in the days it had been a station on the stage line, it had been as crowded on occasion. But certainly not since. The wives and old lady sat at the table, with the smallest children spoon fed on laps. I sat in the other chair. The farmers and their children sat on the floor, scattered around the room gobbling up stew and munching on biscuits. I suspected every plate and bowl and spoon in the place was in use.

With the stew all consumed down to the gravy smears on the plates, the woman made a circuit of the room, passing out squares of molasses cake—the concoction I had watched her stir up earlier. The children, especially, delighted in the dessert. The farmers were not far behind in their enthusiasm.

The older children occupied the younger ones, and the women cleaned up the supper mess while the men and I negotiated prices on the foodstuffs set aside by the wives. I offered the farmers a drink, but they informed me they did not imbibe. We bargained back and forth for a time and settled on a sum more generous than I would have accepted in most situations.

We finished long past nightfall, and some of the children were already asleep, curled in the arms of others. I suggested they turn in and save the packing for morning. The families trooped out the door, and I shuffled to the bedroom, pulled off my boots, and flopped onto the bed, asleep within minutes.

The sleep, such as it was, did not last. I awakened repeatedly,

196

restless and overwrought, jarred from sleep by daunting dreams I could not even remember. I gave up long before dawn streaked the eastern sky and sat at the table sipping coffee sweetened with rum.

The famers were up before the sun, loading and rearranging the loads in the wagons. I lit a lantern to signal I was awake so they would not hesitate to fetch the food supplies inside. When they came, the farmers were spry, in contrast to my bleary eyes and foggy mind. I carried a mug of coffee out to the yard, hoping fresh air would clear my head and improve my disposition.

Just before the loading finished, the woman came carrying a powder box. She handed it to one of the wives, who looked at it and at the woman with questioning eyes. The woman lifted the lid to reveal a box filled nearly to the rim with rice. The farm wife again looked at the woman, wanting an answer.

The woman reached a hand into the box, fingering down into the kernels and coming up with an egg. She had packed eggs in the rice for safe travel. A wide smile lit up the face of the Indiana woman. She turned and handed the box off to the other wife, then enveloped the woman in an enthusiastic embrace. The she grasped the woman's shoulders, held her at arm's length, smiling all the while, then pulled her close in another hug.

When the wagons rolled away, the woman had yet to move. Her dark eyes glistened in the soft morning light. I watched her watching the wagons shrink into the distance.

"Get your ass inside and fix me some breakfast."

A few days later, the letter carrier came through on his way to the mining towns. He stopped only long enough for water and had little to say. He rode away slowly, stopping to look down the old well. He studied the yard, as if making note of any and every change since his last visit.

One of these days, I realized, I would have to do something

about that nosy bastard. He might soon get a closer look at what is down that well than he would like.

Late the next afternoon, a wagon drawn by four mules came over the saddleback pass and jingled and rattled its way down the slant and across the flat. The driver carried a bullwhip, snaking it out from time to time to crack and pop above the ears of his teams. The mules dripped sweat, and lather lined the harness collars.

The driver stood on the wagon as he neared where I stood between the road and the windmill. He hauled back on the lines to stop the mules, propped one foot on the footboard, gathered the lines and whip in one hand, and with the other pulled a flask from his vest pocket and took a sip before speaking. "I hear tell a man has to pay for water here."

I nodded but said nothing.

"How much?"

"A quarter apiece for your mules. A dime for you."

"That's what I heard. Couldn't believe it when I heard it, but that's what I heard." He sipped from the flask, shook it, but heard no sloshing in response. He put the flask back in his pocket, coiled his whip, and rested that hand on his raised thigh. "Anybody ever challenge you on that?"

"Most everyone does."

"Ain't you worried somebody's goin' to kill you for it?"

I shrugged. "A few have attempted violence. They were repaid in kind."

"You think a drink of water is worth killin' a man over?"

"I think no such thing. The water is mine. It comes at a price. Those who do not want to pay the price are welcome to move along. Should they decide, instead, that the prospect of a drink of water is worth dying for, that is not my responsibility."

The muleskinner sat down on the wagon seat and tipped his hat back on his head. The low-hanging sun illuminated his face, but the glare did not seem to concern him.

"You are driving these mules hard," I said.

"That ain't none of your affair. Besides which, mules is meant to work. They get feed and water for their trouble. Ain't nothin' else they need."

I smiled. "They do look as if they need a drink. And I need a dollar if you intend to give it to them at my windmill."

"I guess you don't give me no choice. Any reason I can't park my wagon hereabouts for the night? Or is there a price for that, too?"

"Unhitch anywhere you care to. Put the mules in one of the pens, if you wish. There is a fire ring there in the yard where travelers such as yourself generally set up camp."

I turned to lead him to the yard. I flinched when the bullwhip cracked, but the muleskinner was only putting his teams into motion. He followed along and, after stopping, climbed down and pulled a dollar coin from his vest pocket and flipped it into the air in my direction.

Slipping the caught coin into my pocket, I asked if he would be drinking.

"I have a mighty thirst. But I won't be pourin' no water on it. I expect you got somethin' better to drink, don't you?"

"Whiskey—corn and rye. Rum. Bottled beer, but it is not cold. Coffee."

He set about unhitching and unharnessing the teams and went about his business like a man who knew what he was doing.

"Where are you bound? If you do not mind my asking."

"California."

"Taking up a farm there, are you?"

He laughed. "Oh, hell no. Take a look in the wagon."

I stepped around behind and pulled the cover aside. Everything I could see in the wagon was made of metal, some of it gray, some tinged with rust. There looked to be two halves of a tank of some kind, one nested in the other. There were pipes and rods, wheels and gears, and other parts and pieces. The only thing not made of metal, it seemed, were coils of thick, tightly wound oiled rope.

The muleskinner stood beside me, the mules now free of harness and haltered, lead ropes in his hand. "Well, what do you think?"

"I do not know what to make of it," I said, shaking my head.

He laughed. "That there is a steam donkey."

I did not have to ask what he meant. He read the question on my face.

"Leastways it is when it's all put together. See, a steam donkey—some calls it a donkey engine—is a machine some feller figured out not long ago. Don't see many of 'em around yet, but you will."

"What does it do?"

"What it is, is a winch. Run by a steam engine. Feller what invented it, built it to skid logs for a timber outfit. It'll drag logs six ways to Sunday."

I mulled over what he said. "So you are in the logging business, then?"

"Oh, no. That's just where it come from. I work for a minin' outfit. We ain't a big outfit—mostly just develop claims and sell 'em off to the syndicates. We been usin' the donkey like a hoist. Shaft in our mine weren't deep enough to need a regular hoist, so we used this here machine to lift ore and muck out of the hole and lower equipment and such down."

"You will do the same in California?"

"Hope to. We got a claim there that looks to be a good one." He pulled the wagon cover back where it belonged. "I'd best get these mules watered."

"When you are finished, come on inside. There is a washstand there by the door—water and a towel to dry off with, but no soap."

He jerked the lead ropes harder than was needful and, when one mule jerked back, he lashed out with the tail end of one of the leads and raised a welt across its forehead and face.

The muleskinner did not stop to wash up before coming inside. But the sheen on his face, water droplets on his whiskers, and wet spots on his neckerchief said he must have splashed his face at the trough. I would not be surprised had he taken a drink, as well, but said nothing. I would make up for the loss with the whiskey I was confident he would drink.

I asked if he wanted supper. He said his thirst outweighed his hunger. He stood at the bar, and I poured him three glasses of whiskey, and he emptied them about as fast as I could refill them. The next glass he sipped more slowly, taking the time to actually taste what he drank. He carried the next over to the table and sat.

"I reckon I could stand somethin' to eat now that I've cut the dust and wet it down."

The woman came when I hollered. She sliced him some bread and a piece of cold ham and filled a plate with beans. A sour pickle and brined egg rounded out the fare. He seemed content with it. At least he did not complain. It could be a steady diet of liquor had burnt any other taste out of his mouth. I gave up refilling his glass as he ate and put the bottle down before him. Not long after, I opened a fresh bottle for him.

The muleskinner poured down so much whiskey I decided his legs must be hollow to hold it all. He pushed back from the table and stood—or tried to—and flopped back into the chair. He took a deep breath, grasped the edge of the table with both hands, and pushed himself upright. After swaying for a long moment, he found his equilibrium, more or less. He picked up the bottle—he had long since abandoned the glass—and walked carefully across the room to look at the photographs hanging on the wall. He asked how we came to have the pictures, and I told him about the photographer who visited.

"I had a picture made once." He belched, made a sour face, and swallowed hard, swaying as he stood. "It was one of them little tintypes they make."

"What happened to it?"

He belched again. "Gave it to this girl I knew. Then she went and run off with a gamblin' man. Bitch." Another long swallow from the bottle. "Been a long time since I had me a woman." Another drink. "Say—that woman that was out here. She don't look like much, but you know what they say."

"What is it that they say?"

"They all look the same in the dark." He laughed at his joke. "Is it all right if I go on back there through that curtain and take a ride?"

I named a price.

He considered it. "Aw, what the hell—it's only money." With the bottle dangling from the end of his arm, he shuffled and staggered his way back to and through the curtain. I heard him yell something at the woman, then again, then nothing for a few minutes. The next sound was a gurgling scream.

I thrust the curtain aside and ducked through. By the dim light of a candle on the bedside table, I could see the muleskinner upright on his knees astraddle the woman. She did her best to yell and scream as he slapped her repeatedly with his palm and the back of his hand, arm swinging like an unbalanced and jerky pendulum. The whiskey bottle stood on the table next to the candle. I grasped it by the neck and picked it up, noting by its heft it still contained a good deal of the drink, lending it weight and substance.

His hand struck the woman again, the sound of it lost in the shatter and splash as the bottle caved in the back of his head.

The muleskinner slumped forward, and I grabbed a handful of shirt collar and vest and jerked him upright and off the bed.

The woman scooted into the corner of the bed and would have faded through the walls had she been able. Her eyes were wide and anxious. Trickles of blood traced paths from flared nostrils to her lips. The skin around one eye was already swollen, and a dark patch covered one cheek. As I watched her, she drew the blanket up around her and wormed deeper into the corner. I reached around the muleskinner and lifted him up to sit on the bed, then draped him over my shoulder.

With both hands on the rock rim of the well, I gasped to catch my breath as I listened to him bounce against the sides of the well as he fell, then the sound of his body landing at the bottom.

The cabin sits cold and dark. Chimney stands breathless, exhaling no smoke. No light glows against the dusk. Door hangs askew on sagged boot-sole hinges. No dog barks. No milk cow lows.

The rider sits muleback on the rise. Aching for home. For the wife and infant who await. He watches. He rides downslope in fits and starts. Stopping, waiting for something to change. But like a faded daguerreotype of a homestead frozen in time, nothing nor no one on his claim answers his call.

Saddle leather groans as he steps down. Pats the mule on the shoulder. Rein slides from his hand, slithering to the dust in the dooryard. He pulls free an arrow embedded in the door and tosses it away. He presses palm to plank and pushes. The door resists, its swing lopsided from violence. He pushes harder; the door gouges across the floor. He steps inside and stands aside, awaiting the seeing of his eyes to adjust to the emptiness of nightfall. He sees nothing.

He follows his memory across the room to the cookstove. A leg strikes a leg of an overturned chair. Hands pat the stove shelf, find a box of matches where it does not belong. He swipes matchstick across stovetop, and a halo of light surrounds him. He holds the flame up, sees a lantern on the floor, its chimney fractured fragments, its oil a spilled stain.

Another match, and a candle comes to hand. Circumnavigating tipped table and upended chairs, he steps through strewn debris, following the light in his hand to the corner of the cabin where he—they—sleep. He sees her hands, tied to the bedframe. Viscous blood, puddled beneath fingertips. Face turned away. The crown of her head a rough red patch, droplets of blood reflecting the light. Her arms encased in the sleeves of a dress no longer there. A long red slash separates naked breasts, the split disappearing in the gore between her thighs.

He turns away, hoists the candle high, casts feeble light through the darkness. Runnels of wax blister his clenched fist. There is no baby. No baby.

He uprights a chair and sits, hands hanging free. The candle gutters out.

CHAPTER TWENTY-FOUR

The sun rose without me the next day. It was well up in the morning sky when I struggled to wake. I took some coffee but had no stomach for breakfast. I shuffled out to the yard to look the situation over. I pulled the cover off the muleskinner's wagon, then harnessed and hitched two of his mules—hoping they were a team, and the wheelers at that—and used them to move the wagon. I backed it up to an open shed, a lean-to attached to the side of one of the outbuildings full of this and that I had no present use for. The metal parts and pieces of the steam donkey should be safe enough in the open air. Besides, I was not sure how I would get the largest pieces off the wagon, let alone through a doorway.

By the time I had everything I could lift unloaded and stowed, two horsemen reined up and watched me shift a gear shaft onto the pile of parts. I stepped out from behind the wagon and saw the visitors were the woman's uncle and his son, or whatever relation the boy was that I could not properly recall. Wiping the sweat from my face and forehead with a shirtsleeve, I walked over and stood before the scrawny horses they rode. They said nothing, only stared at me with clenched jaws and tight lips.

I took another swipe at the runnels of sweat dripping off my chin and cheeks. "To what do I owe the pleasure of your company this day?"

The boy looked at the man, then turned to me. "We need money. Our allotments from the government are used up. As usual, we were not given what was promised. We are here to see if there is work."

"Tend to your horses. Then help me finish unloading this wagon."

The uncle was still fit and strong despite his gray-shot hair and narrow frame. The boy had the confidence of youth beyond his physical ability. Between the three of us, we got the heavy halves of the tank off the wagon, as well as the weighty drums and gears. We sat in the shade cooling off while I contemplated what to do next.

I looked at the two mules, standing hipshot in harness, and the other pair in the pen across the yard. Four mules showing up at once in my corrals might attract undue attention— particularly from that letter hauler and his damnable curiosity.

"Those cattle you drove to the fort for me. Do you remember that?"

The old man nodded.

"You recall where you met me to take over the herd?"

Another nod.

I had deliberately met them on the trail out in the valley, well away from the box canyon where I concealed my livestock, out of fear they would steal from me, as the woman's brothers had done. But, wanting to deal with the wagon and not wanting to leave the place at present, I decided to risk passing along the knowledge.

"Not far from there, there is a narrow cleft in the mountains to the west. It opens into a hidden canyon, where there is water and grass."

The boy looked at the man, who gave no sign he even heard me, let alone understood.

"I keep stock in there—a few oxen, a few beeves, and some horses. I want you to take these mules there."

The man's expression did not change.

"If I were to draw you a map, do you think you could find that canyon?"

Now, the man's eyes twinkled, and his mouth twitched with the hint of a smile, which he did not allow to develop. He turned to the boy and jabbered away in Paiute. When he finished talking, the boy turned to me.

"He says our people have known of that place for as long as the sky has been blue. It is hidden only in your mind."

I let that settle for a time. Then, "Will you take these mules there and turn them loose? And, while you are there, look over the other stock and see they are well?"

The old man nodded, then said something more to the boy.

"He wants to know how much you will pay for this."

I named a price, and he declined. I upped the offer, and still he would not accept. My third overture met his approval. Likely so, as it was well beyond the value of less than a day's work. But that was not the end of it. The man said something more to the boy.

"He says you owe us for the work with the wagon."

"Like hell I do! You will accept what we agreed on as payment for all the work, or you can ride out of here empty handed. Try to feed your families with that."

They talked back and forth and finally consented to accept the amount offered.

"You will not be paid until you come back here."

The old man nodded his assent. The two of them unhitched the mules, choused the other two out of the corral, mounted their ponies, and drove the mules to the trough at the windmill to let them and their horses drink, then rode off to the north to meet the trail.

The work had given me an appetite, and I went inside to see what the woman had to feed me. Her face looked a wreck. Dried blood crusted her nostrils, and fresh blood still seeped out, sponged away as it did with a rag more red than white. One eye was swollen shut, the swelling shades of red and purple. Other bruises patterned her cheeks and jaw. I thought it fortunate her uncle had not seen her and gotten the wrong idea.

Or, perhaps he had, and the woman told him the truth of the matter. If so, I hoped her telling had not included the disposition of her assailant.

She shuffled around at the stove, frying bacon and eggs, slicing bread to toast on the stove, and topping off the coffeepot. I ate like a man famished from a long lack of food—a decided difference from my appetite earlier in the day.

Back out in the yard, I walked around the muleskinner's wagon and decided there was nothing distinctive enough about it to cause concern. The wheels had once been red and yellow, but the paint was flaked, faded, and abraded enough to be barely noticeable. The only thing left in the bed was a jumble of camp equipment. Everything was battered and worn and of no value, so down the well it went to rejoin its owner. The muleskinner did not even carry a proper bedroll, only a wad of fetid blankets that raised a foul-smelling smoke when burned. The jockey box contained a whiskey bottle with an inch or so in the bottom, a few tools, and a leather purse with a bit of money.

I pulled the bows from the staples and leaned them into the stack with others of their kind. I removed and stored all the hitching apparatus. The harnesses, from bridles to breeching, went into the barn to hang. Finally, I picked up the tongue and pushed the wagon into line with the others.

By then, the sun was down. As I washed up, the woman's uncle and the boy came back. A mule deer carcass draped across the bows of the old man's saddle. The meat would help stem the hunger of his family for a bit. The boy said, with a snide sort of smile, that they had found my secret canyon without difficulty. He said they had turned the mules loose and rode through the rest of the herd to assure everything was all right, which it was.

The woman fed us a supper of beans and biscuits doused with gravy, and venison steaks carved from the deer. She exchanged hand signs with her uncle. He cast suspicious glances my way from time to time, but she apparently persuaded him I was not responsible for her injuries, which looked even uglier than they had earlier.

The man and boy intended to leave before daylight. They took the leftover biscuits in a cloth bag, the better part of a ham, some canned goods the woman had sacked up, and retired to sleep in the yard.

It was quiet on the road for the next couple of days. Then the man who carried the mail came by, on his way back to the settlements from the mining towns. I stepped out of the barn and watched him.

As usual, he stopped by the old well and looked to see if anything had changed. Which, of course, it had—but the changes were well beyond his seeing. The he took a turn through the wagon yard. I had some trouble controlling my breathing when he stopped to study the muleskinner's wagon. I walked out to meet him.

He greeted me with his half nod. "That a new wagon?"

"Not so much new as rebuilt. Put it together from parts I had on hand. Cannot say how many broken-down wagons I took parts from to assemble it. It will make a suitable wagon for someone, I trust."

The man stared at me for an uncomfortable time. "It's gettin' late in the day. May as well stay over. I'll water the horse, then wash up and come on inside if that's all right with you. Maybe have a bottle of that beer you got—if you still got any, that is."

I said that was fine with me. And that he could drink beer as long as his money lasted, but I reminded him it was not cold.

As he sipped his first bottle of beer, he stood before the hanging photograph of himself beside the old well, astride his horse. He studied the picture for a long time, as if he expected to see something different in it than had been there before.

The woman fixed us a supper of venison steaks left over from her uncle's visit, fried up with the last of the potatoes and onions from the root cellar. And she stirred up a batch of boiled rice with cinnamon, sugar, canned milk, and raisins. As he ate, the mail carrier nursed his beer and, when that was finished, asked for coffee. We sat and sipped and made small talk.

"Some over in them minin' towns thinks they might be gettin' close to another vein of color. Leastways, they say there's signs. Most of 'em, though, say it'll peter out like all the rest of 'em has done lately. Some more folks packed up and headed for California since last I was there. Had to send a few letters on."

I topped off our coffee mugs and spooned up another bowl of the rice pudding and ate as we talked. "There have been few coming by on the road going east—I guess all those abandoning the mines of late are choosing to go to California."

"Seems like." He asked for a splash of rum to sweeten his coffee, and I fetched a bottle. "Seen many folks comin' from the east of late?"

"Not many. Two families came by a while back. Farmers, from Indiana, they said. Wanting to try their luck in California. Their luck had not been so good, so far. Lost a good share of their supplies when a wagon caught fire and burned."

He nodded. "I saw that burnt-out wagon. By that little spring a couple days east of here. Wondered what happened."

"I outfitted them with a wagon. Resupplied them with food."

The mail carrier sipped his sweetened coffee, then smiled. I suspected there was little mirth in the smile, and my suspicions proved correct when he spoke. "I imagine you charged them farmers a pretty penny, too."

I said nothing for a time, letting my anger seethe, then dissipate somewhat. Then, through clenched teeth, "They paid my price."

He laughed, also without humor. "It ain't like they had much choice, is it? They had to pay your price or starve."

Swallowing a long sip of coffee to calm myself, I stood and poured my mug full again before responding. All I could think to say was, "You think ill of me."

"Well, hell, it ain't no wonder! Any man who makes thirsty folks pay for water in this desert ain't got no love but for money. A man like you'd pinch a penny so hard your thumb is likely to poke a hole right through it."

For a few long minutes I sat and pondered the possibility of giving the man a good look at what was down that old well he was always so curious about. But I thought better of it—or, at least I changed my mind—and left him sitting at the table alone when I walked back to the bedroom and pushed my way through the curtain.

He was gone when I came back through the curtain in the morning. The rum bottle still stood on the table, along with his empty coffee mug and beer bottle. A precise stack of coins, enough to cover his food and drink and water for his horse, also stood there. I swept up the money and deposited it in the money box under the store counter and stepped outside to visit the backhouse. I looked toward the saddleback pass just in time to see a rider, silhouetted against the dawn sky, top out and disappear over the summit.

It was only four days later when he came back. This time, there were two other riders with him. One was the United States marshal who had come through here looking for the bank robber. The other man, younger, also had a marshal's badge pinned to his chest.

CHAPTER TWENTY-FIVE

The three horsemen rode directly into the yard. The man who carried the mail reined up in front of the muleskinner's wagon and dismounted. The marshal I had met before and the other one, a deputy, I assumed, stepped down as well. I walked over to join them.

"Can I be of assistance to you gentlemen?"

The marshal said, "Yessir. It seems there is a question as to the origin of this wagon—this is the wagon you meant, ain't it?" he said to the mail carrier, who said it was.

"What question could there possibly be? I built this wagon from parts of other salvaged wagons."

"That ain't so," the man who carried the mail said. "I seen this wagon. Passed it on the road goin' west my last trip. Driven by a man with four mules in harness. Stopped and talked with him for a bit."

"I saw that man. He came through here. Did not stop any longer than it took to water his mules."

"And I suppose you charged him a dollar to do it."

"Damn right I did. So what?"

The marshal raised a hand to still us. "Enough." He turned to the mail man. "How do you know this is the wagon you saw? It looks like most any wagon to me."

The letter carrier walked to the offside of the wagon, and we followed. He pointed to the front wheel. "See this wheel here?

See how it's been painted—used to be a red rim with yellow spokes?"

We all could see what he meant, despite the scarcity of paint yet left on the wheel.

"Now, looky here—you can see where them two spokes has been replaced. See? The new ones ain't got a trace of paint on 'em. I noticed that, when I was talkin' to the driver on the road. Squatted down next to that wheel, lookin' right at it, I was, when we talked."

The marshal looked the wheel over, as did the deputy. My stomach roiled, and my mind reeled, wondering how I could have overlooked those unpainted spokes.

"The man's got a point," the marshal said to me. "What do you have to say for yourself?"

I swallowed hard. "I would have to say it is all nonsense. That man and his mules and his wagon came by, just like I said. And he kept going, just like I said."

The mail man scoffed. "Like hell. I never seen him on the road when I was comin' back. And I never saw nor heard of his bein' in any of them mine towns, neither. It ain't like he could disappear." He stabbed a finger toward the wheel. "I tell you, that's his wagon. And if it ain't his wagon, it's sure as hell his wheel."

The young lawman slipped slowly around behind me. The marshal tipped his hat back with his forefinger and said, "Well, seems to me there's somethin' to answer for here." He turned toward the road, casting his eyes about and stopping when he found the old well. "Seems there's a question concerning that old well yonder, too."

The three of them mounted their horses and rode to the well. I walked along behind them. Without being asked, the deputy stepped down and leaned over the rock rim. He drew back quickly.

"He's right. Sure as hell stinks like somethin's dead down there."

The marshal reined his horse around until he faced me. "What do you have to say about that?"

I laughed. Or tried to. "It is no wonder to me that it stinks. We throw all manner of trash down there. Manure. Kitchen trash. Guts and carcasses from deer or cattle we kill. Of course it stinks." I nodded toward the mail man. "That one there, he seems to like the smell of it. Sticks his nose in it every time he comes by."

"He has his suspicions of what's down there, and it ain't just trash. What with that wagon, and other things I have heard about this place, I reckon it's worth havin' a look."

I stood upright and took in a sudden breath. "What is it you intend to do?"

The marshal said nothing. But all three of the men took down coiled ropes tied to their saddle horns. I saw they were not catch ropes such as cowboys used in their work. This was new rope, with no hondas tied in to build loops.

"We'll need a light," the marshal said.

The mail man said he knew there were lanterns in the roadhouse and left at a fast walk to fetch one. While he was gone, the deputy tied the ends of two of the ropes together.

The marshal said, "Give me that." He untied the knot and looped the rope ends around and about and through one another by some illusory method, then pulled them tight. "That knot," he said, "is called a Flemish bend. Learned it from my granddaddy. It ain't likely to come undone." He tied on the other rope the same way and snake-coiled the lengthened rope onto the ground next to the well.

Carrying one of my coal-oil lanterns in his hand, the mail man came back from the roadhouse. He set the lantern on the rock rim, then thought better of it and put it on the ground. He took a match from a box that looked to have come off my store shelves and lit the lantern.

The marshal showed the deputy how to tie a bowline knot around himself and advised him to wrap his bandana around his nose, warning that the stink would likely get a lot worse the further he got down the well.

Stepping across and sitting on the rim, the deputy held onto the rope with one hand and used the other to snug his hat down tight around his ears and to adjust the bandana. He picked up the lantern and swallowed hard. "I'm countin' on you two."

"Don't you fret none, boy," the marshal said. "We won't let you go. Just be careful not to scrape your hide off on the sides as you go down."

With that, the marshal and the mail carrier leaned back on the rope, the lawman wrapping it half around his backside for leverage, and the deputy swung his other leg over the rim and started sliding slowly down, the rope scratching stone as the men fed it out hand over hand.

It seemed to me a long, long time later when the rope went slack.

It did not take long before the rope jerked. Three times. The marshal now sat his horse, and the mail man handed him the rope. He tied it off on his saddlehorn with a double half hitch, turned the horse around, and rode slowly away from the well. The mail man stood at the rim, watching the rope slide over the stones, and helped one of the hitches ride over without snagging.

The young lawman's head emerged, and with both hands atop the wall he pushed himself over, draped by his waist. He hung there for a short while, gasping. He slung a leg over and rolled off, rolled to his back, and kept sucking in air.

"Where the hell is my good lantern?"

The marshal hushed me with a look.

But the deputy answered, spitting out words between heaving breaths. "Left it down there. Went out. Not enough air. To keep it burning."

After a few minutes, the deputy rolled over and levered himself up to sit, his back against the well wall. He reached inside his vest and pulled out a soiled rag.

"That's it!" the mail man said. "That's the man's bandana! I saw it, wrapped around his throat."

I said, "Nonsense! That is just an old rag the woman threw out. Could have come from anywhere."

"Nope," the young officer said. "I took it off of a man down there. Just like he said. It's a neck scarf. Or was."

The marshal squatted down in front of the other lawman and tipped his hat back. "So you're sayin' that there is a body down there. For certain."

"Yep. And more'n one. I kicked aside some trash 'fore the light went out. Uncovered some legs. And I believe I saw another somebody, but I ain't sure—the lamp went out."

The marshal stood, his knees popping as he did. He walked to his horse, unbuckled the flap on a saddlebag, and pulled a set of handcuffs from inside. He wrenched one of my arms behind me and snapped on the cuff, then jerked the other arm behind.

"There is no need for that," I said. "Just put the damn cuffs on me. You do not need to break my arms doing it." I asked why he cuffed me behind, and he allowed that I was a wily one and would likely be less trouble bound that way.

Pulling a clasp knife from his pocket, the marshal sawed off a couple of short lengths from the end of the long rope. He shoved me toward the yard and followed, pushing me along every few steps. The others came along behind. The marshal stopped me at the fence around the big corral, stuck a booted foot behind my legs, and shoved me to the ground.

"I said there is no need for that! Since I am not resisting, rough treatment is hardly necessary."

"Shut up." He wrapped the rope around the base of the corner post, threaded it through the chain on the handcuffs, and knotted it. He took care to slide the knot around to the back of the post, beyond my reach. Then he wrapped the other piece of rope around and around my ankles, pulled it tighter than need be, and tied it off.

The three men stepped away and squatted in a circle. They talked for quite some time, out of my hearing.

After a while, after whatever they had to say had been said, the circle broke apart. The marshal mounted his horse and rode around to the roadhouse. The other two led their mounts to the small pen by the barn, unsaddled them, and turned them in to the corral. They started for the roadhouse.

"Hey! You cannot leave me here!" Both men stopped, turned, looked at me, then turned away and started walking. "Hey! I could use a drink of water!"

They stopped again and looked at me. "Shut up," the mail man said. "Maybe I'll come back later and let you have a drink." He stared at me. "By the way, it'll cost you a dime."

I sat bound in the sun stewing, with no notion of what was going on. After a while, the marshal rode past, spurring his horse into a trot down the road headed west. Later, after the sun went down but before night fell, the young deputy came bearing a plate of food and a glass of water. He set them down, had me shift around, and unlocked the handcuffs. It took me a few minutes to rub feeling back into my hands and wrists, but, once my grip returned, I picked up the water and gulped it down.

"Whoa . . . best take it easy, there, pard. There ain't no more where that came from—well, there is, but that fellow who carries the mail is plumb decided that you ain't gettin' none."

"It is my water, damn it, and I shall drink all I please."

He smiled. "I reckon so—long as you can get to it from here. 'Cause it's certain sure you ain't movin' from this place."

I started in on the food—leftovers from what the woman had cooked earlier—forking up mouthfuls and swallowing before they were fully chewed. It is an odd thing how sitting on your ass in the sun for the better part of a day doing nothing can work up an appetite in a man.

I swallowed another bite and thought it best to take a pause unless everything that went down decided to come back up. "What is it you are planning to do?"

The lawman looked over each shoulder, as if to assure himself no one would overhear. As if that would matter. "The boss, he's gone on to them towns in the mountains. Me, I'm to stay here and keep an eye on you. The other fellow, well, he can do as he pleases, but he's determined to stay here. Says it will be a pleasure to watch you get yours."

"My what?"

"Don't rightly know. But that's what he said—said you'll get yours."

After a few more bites of food, I asked him what the marshal intended to do in the mining towns.

"Well, the way he put it was, we ain't got the wherewithal to get up what's down that well. Says it ain't that much different than minin', so he's fixin' to fetch some miners."

I laughed. "Just what the hell is it you all think they are going to find down there?"

He drew back slightly, and his eyebrows drew together as he looked at me. "Can't rightly say what all they'll find. But, from what I saw, there's dead folks down there. And that mail man swears they didn't fall in on their own."

"Well, we shall see. We shall see."

The deputy took the plate from me. I shook out the last drops of water in the glass onto my tongue, then handed it to him. He set them aside and bent to attach the fetters. My elbow met the side of his head with as much strength as I could muster. The blow tipped the deputy over, and he kept rolling out of reach and was back on his feet before I could get to him, handicapped as I was by my bound feet. He kicked out, and the toe of his boot landed under my chin, snapping my head back.

I remember nothing more of the night.

Chapter Twenty-Six

The same boot that put me down for the night woke me up in the morning. Prodding me with his toe, the young deputy kept poking until I rolled from my side to my back, propped myself on my elbows to look around through squinted eyes, then sat up.

The abuse the night before resulted, somehow, in a restful night. I felt refreshed, my sleep undisturbed by those troublesome, unremembered dreams that upset my waking hours as well as those of the night.

"Are you going to remove these damnable handcuffs?"

"Why should I?"

"Good Lord, man! I need to visit the backhouse! Surely you do not expect me to fester here in my own water. That is uncivilized."

"What about this?"

For the first time I looked up at the lawman. In his hands were a plate and a coffee mug.

"It will keep."

He looked from the plate to the mug and back again, then looked around for a place to put them, and stepped away and set them on the ground under the fence rail. "Lay down," he said. "On your belly."

I did as he ordered and waited while he untied my feet and the rope tying the handcuffs to the corner post. I felt him fiddling with the shackles, assuming he was unlocking them.

"Roll over," he said. "And don't try anything funny." Then, "Lift up your hands."

He locked on the cuffs again, this time with my hands in front. With pistol drawn and pointed at my face, he ordered me to get up, then followed me to the backhouse, staying a step or two behind, just out of reach should I decide to swing around and attack. The deputy was young, but obviously not stupid. Or, at the least, he was a fast learner.

Back at the corral post, he sat me down with a shove and tied my ankles together. The plate he handed me held only a pile of scrambled eggs in congealed grease.

"What is this?"

"It's your breakfast. What the hell do you think?"

"No meat? No bread?"

He shrugged. "It's what the other feller cooked. That woman of yours—seems she don't want to cook for us."

I smiled. "That right?"

"Seems so. She ain't said nothin'. She ain't even come out of that back room." He lifted his hat and scratched his head. "Guess it don't mean nothin' that she ain't talked—he says she can't talk—ain't got no tongue."

I nodded. "He is right."

"Said it got cut out. Says he wouldn't be surprised if it was you what did it."

I said nothing, just poked and prodded at the eggs with the fork, decided if this was all there was to eat, I had best eat it. It was not easy. The coffee was not any more palatable than the eggs—lukewarm and bitter. I drank it down and handed the mug and plate to the deputy. "Send the woman out here. I do not care if she will not cook for you—but she will sure as hell cook for me. I will not tolerate such fare as this."

The day passed without incident. I sat bound to the corral post like a recalcitrant horse left to soak in the sun and think about its bad behavior. Along about the middle of the afternoon, the man who carried the mail came out with the kitchen bucket and a drinking glass. He walked to the windmill and filled the bucket from the pipe, then made a show of filling the glass and drinking down the fresh water. He looked my way, refilled the glass, sloshed it around to rinse, dumped it, and refilled it. Then he came my way, stopped just out of reach, and put down the bucket.

"Thirsty?"

I nodded, and he stepped closer and handed me the glass.

"No charge."

I drank the water down and handed him back the empty glass. "I have yet to have my dinner."

"Same with me. But your wife is fixing supper. It took some talkin', but I reckon she finally came to know it would take too long to starve you to death."

I realized he was probably right—the woman's refusal to cook was more likely the result of my not being in a position to punish her for it, than her not wanting to cook for my captors. I would take that up with her at the first opportunity.

Sometime in the night I woke up drenched with sweat despite the chill of the high desert air. The cause of my disturbance was yet another forgotten dream. I contemplated raising a ruckus and persuading the lawman to again render me unconscious. The still-throbbing bruise on my chin, which I could not massage given the fetters that bound me, convinced me otherwise. Instead, I curled in as much of a ball as my situation allowed and awaited the day and the sun that would first warm, then overheat me.

The marshal must have ridden straight through to and from the mining towns, for he returned late in the day. He rode straight to me, and I could see in the dark circles under his eyes and sagging flesh of his face that he was spent.

He watched me for a minute from the saddle. "How you holdin' up?"

"Better than you are, from the look of it."

"I'll be all right. Night's sleep will do wonders for me."

"Since you are alone, I assume you have failed in your mission."

He shook his head. "Not so. I rode ahead, but there's a wagon loaded with tools and three miners right behind me. Be here 'fore you know it." He stepped down from his horse.

"Just what is it you intend for these miners of yours to do—if you do not mind my asking."

"Not at all. They are goin' to bring enough evidence up out of that well to hang you."

I smiled. "And just how will they go about it?"

He shrugged. "I ain't got no idea. That'll be up to them. But when I told 'em the situation, they acted like it wouldn't be no trouble." He rubbed his face and scoured his eyes. "Hardest part was convincin' 'em to come. Seems things is pickin' up in one of them mines—looks like they're findin' more ore than they have been."

With a foot-dragging shuffle, he led his horse to the barn and into the bay, unsaddled and brushed it down, and turned it into the small corral and set out a bucket of my oats. He went to the roadhouse, and soon the deputy came out and carried the horse a bucket of water.

While he was at it, the wagon rolled in.

The miners parked the wagon not far from me, and one of them unhitched the team and walked them to the trough to water. I made a mental note that fifty cents was due me. The other two walked out to the old well, walked around it, leaned into it, and walked around it some more.

By the time the horses were in the pen, the marshal, the deputy, and the mail man came out. The marshal carried a mug of coffee, and it looked to have revived him somewhat. They gathered with the miners at the wagon.

"Well, what do you think?" the marshal said to the miners.

"Oh, we can get down there all right," one said. "Tight quarters. Have to do it one man at a time. Place stinks like a gut pile."

"Wait till you get down there," the deputy said. "It was all I could do to keep from pukin'. It didn't help none that there ain't much air down there. I couldn't hardly get a breath. Not even enough air to keep the lantern lit."

"Our cap lamps don't need much air to keep the oil burning—smaller flame than a lantern. We might could burn a candle spike or two, too."

Another of the miners said, "First thing we got to figure out is how to get up and down the hole. Have to put up some kind of a headframe. Maybe hang a block and use the team to lift. We'll look around, see what we can scrounge up to build a frame."

I watched the miners wander the yard and in and out of the sheds and buildings, looking for the materials they needed. "Holy shit!" came a shout from one of the miners, out of my line of vision. The other miners hurried to join him while the lawmen and the letter carrier watched from where they stood and squatted next to the wagon. I heard the clank and ring of shifting metal as the miners rummaged around in whatever pile they had found. They were still excited, chattering away as they came to the wagon.

The marshal asked what they had found to cause such an uproar.

"You see that pile over there under that shed? Looks like scrap iron? That there is a donkey engine!"

The marshal and deputy looked at the miner as if he were speaking in some foreign tongue. The marshal was first to speak.

"What the hell is a donkey engine?"

"It's a steam engine and winch. Called a donkey engine, or a steam donkey."

"So?"

"With that there machine, we can hoist stuff up and down that well shaft like nobody's business. Slick as grass through a goose. I run a donkey engine for a time in a mine back in the Black Hills. Had to maintain it, too, so I know them machines inside and out."

The marshal pursed his lips and furrowed his brow, looking at the unassembled mess. "How long will it take to get it goin'?"

"Day or two. No longer."

The marshal thought for a long moment. "We lose a day or two of work, then."

"Not really. We got to put up some kind of headframe, anyway. The others can do that whilst I put the machine together. Besides, even if it takes an extra day, we'll make up for it. It's the best way."

"All right. Get to it." He asked—in a way that was not a question—the deputy and the mail man to help the miners. "Me, I'm goin' to catch up on some sleep."

For two days and nights I sat bound in misery at the corner of the corral. Behind me, the one miner banged and clanged and cussed and carried on as he assembled the steam donkey with a lack of proper tools. In front of me, the rest of my guests pilfered my supply of lumber and iron fixtures, cobbling together a makeshift gallows frame atop the well. Inside the roadhouse, the woman cooked soups and stews by the barrel and baked biscuits by the bushel to fuel the enterprise—all the while diminishing my stores of food.

Late the second day, the steam donkey man declared his work finished. He filled the boiler with water from my windmill, and stuffed the firebox with stove-lengths from my woodpile and set it alight. It built up a head of steam, clanking and knocking and tapping until the pressure was right. The men, one and all—save me—gathered around the donkey engine and raised a cheer when the miner engaged the gears with a clunk, and the drum turned and reversed, feeding out and retracting the rope on the spool as intended. There followed a few short blasts from a steam whistle. Then the miner shut down the engine and announced that he would let it cool off overnight, drag it into position near the well come morning, and put it to work by midday.

And that is just how it unfolded when the sun came up. While the miner harnessed a team and rigged a hitch to the donkey engine frame, the others knocked together a hoisting platform and fashioned a canvas sling from one of my stored wagon covers. I had to admit that, from my vantage point, the operation looked to be an inventive arrangement of skill and experience.

That it had come together with the sole purpose of exposing all my sins, remembered in the bottom of the well, did serve to diminish my admiration somewhat.

"Hey!" I shouted out to the miner standing on the platform waiting to be lowered into the darkness, with shovel and pry bar and other implements standing beside him, wrapped in one arm. "When you get down there, find my lantern and bring it up."

He smiled at me as he disappeared down the hole.

It did not take long for the first body to come up. They laid the muleskinner out on another sheet of my canvas, and the marshal stood, hands on knees, studying the body as the other lawman and the mail man and one of the miners stood by. I could not hear what they said, but I could see them point and talk, roll the body over, and talk some more.

The marshal walked over and squatted in front of me, tipping his hat back with his forefinger. "Want to tell me what happened to that man?"

"I do not have any idea what you are talking about."

"That dead man over there. Seems he is the man who was driving that wagon with the new spokes in the wheel."

I shrugged. "I could not say."

"He looks to have had his head bashed in."

"He was a drinking man. I know that. Perhaps he had too much to drink and fell in the well. He could have hit his head on the side."

The marshal nodded. "Could have, I suppose. Only thing is, where his head is stove in, there is little pieces of glass. Looks like they came off a whiskey bottle."

I shrugged again. "As I said, I do not know what you are talking about."

"Still and all, it don't look good for you, far as I'm concerned. You might as well tell me the truth."

He realized after a time that I had no more to say and returned to the well.

About the time he got there, two Paiutes—the woman's uncle and the boy—rode up and stopped where they could watch the activity at the well. They sat for a few minutes, then the old man said something to the boy, and he turned and went back the way they had come. The old man did not move, just sat his horse and watched. Later, he corralled his horse, rolled out a blanket, and sat. He watched as the day faded and was still watching when the sun went down and the platform and sling came up another time. The miner stepped off the platform onto the rim, then helped retrieve the dangling sling as it cleared the wall. Inside, I knew, would be the body of the drover on his way home to Arkansas.

If the miners kept at their work, it would not be the last body they would find.

Chapter Twenty-Seven

The faintest hint of dawn glowed in the east when the clanging and banging of the miner filling the firebox on the steam donkey awakened me. I rolled onto my back and stared at the stars broadcast across the dark sky and traced the bow of the milky way along its path. Dawn spread and stars faded, and metal knocked and rattled as steam pressure built in the tank.

I elbowed my way up to sit. I looked around and could barely make out the woman's uncle, sitting in the same place he sat yesterday, as if he had not moved. Soon, the other two miners came from the roadhouse, the marshal close behind. He diverged from their path and came to me, bearing a mug and a plate. He set them aside, grabbed me by a shoulder and jerked me around to unlock the cuffs. He refastened them with my hands in front so I could eat.

The marshal squatted before me in the dim light and tipped his hat back with a forefinger to the brim. "You got anything to say for yourself?"

I shook my head while chewing a mouthful of biscuit.

"You sure?"

I swallowed. "I cannot think of what I might say that would matter. Your mind is made up, and you do not appear to be inclined to change it."

"Well, if there's any other explanation for what's in that well, you better say it."

I took another bite of biscuit and shook my head. He stood

and hitched up his pants. "After you're done eatin' we'll be pullin' out."

The stiffness in my neck from sleeping on the cold ground pained me when my head snapped up to look at him. "Pulling out? For where? Why?"

He did not answer. The marshal hitched up his britches once again and walked away. I lowered the plate to my lap and drank off half the mug of coffee at once, then sat and watched the miners at their preparations. As if on cue, all three of them stopped what they were doing and looked to the west. Coming along the road was a string of Indians, Paiutes, some mounted and others afoot. There must have been a dozen of them—a mix of men, women, and children. I recognized the boy who had been here before and had come yesterday with the woman's uncle.

They stopped where the old uncle sat and spread blankets on the ground. Two of the women unrolled poles from a canvas sheet and put up a shade against the coming sun. They unpacked parfleches and baskets, passing around food and drink, and sat watching the miners at their work. This place was getting to looking more like a circus all the time.

I took my time eating. A blast from the steam whistle on the donkey engine startled me so bad I almost upset the plate. The sound brought the mail man, the marshal, and his deputy out of the roadhouse, high-stepping it toward the well. The woman came too but, rather than following the men to the well, she joined the Indians, lowering herself to sit cross-legged among them on a blanket.

All watched as the platform lifted a miner out of the well, the canvas sling swaying beneath with its load. When the sling lowered to the ground, the marshal squatted by the body it carried, studying it for signs of how the man died. Then he and the deputy carried the corpse away and laid it out under the wagon cover with the other bodies.

The marshal walked over to where I sat, the mail man on his heels. He stood over me, a looming silhouette as the sun lifted over the crest of the mountains, casting his shadow over me.

"I am formally placin' you under arrest for murder and whatever else I can think of. I'll be haulin' your sorry ass to the city soon as we can get a team hitched to a wagon. Seein' as it's evidence, we'll be takin' that wagon with the wheel spokes that ain't painted." He turned to the mail carrier. "I'll tend to the wagon if you'll take this reprobate to the backhouse. Meet me at the roadhouse, and we'll pick up the supplies from inside on the way out."

The marshal untied my ankles, grabbed the chain on the shackles, and jerked me to my feet. While he unlatched the cuffs and moved them around front, he asked which of the horses in the corral would make the most likely team. He headed for the barn for halters. The mail man gathered my breakfast dishes and told me to get moving. He kept his distance as we walked to the backhouse.

Later, I sat on the roadhouse step and waited. The wagon pulled up by the door with the two saddle horses tied to the back and the men's saddles in the bed. The mail carrier brought out a box of food and other supplies for the road—from my stores, mind you—and some blankets and slid them into the bed. The marshal told me to climb in the back. He bound my ankles and checked the cuffs on my wrists. We stopped at the windmill to fill a keg and some canteens and let the horses drink their fill.

I sat on the back of the wagon with my legs dangling over the end, jostling and bouncing as we followed the rough road across the sagebrush flat and climbed the slant. I watched the windmill, the roadhouse, and all else I owned in the world grow small. We crossed over the saddleback pass, and I wondered if ever I would see any of it again.

Chapter Twenty-Eight

And now I have sat for months in this cell, moldering away as surely as the bodies in the well. I could have been tried and convicted time and again by now, but the powers that be seem determined to wait, to see how many times they can hang me.

From time to time I am given a newspaper, in the pages of which I am called a monster, a devil, evil incarnate, and all manner of epithets. But, still, I think of myself a businessman, who did his best to make a living—and a future—under difficult conditions. Just how long that future will be, given my present circumstances, is difficult to contemplate.

Few come to see me. A reporter, from time to time, from one of the local newspapers, or a correspondent from more distant publications. But their questions are inane and predictable. The marshal comes by from time to time. He asks, repeatedly, for information about the bodies they recover from the well. He wants to know who, and he wants to when—but he never asks why.

Occasionally, the young deputy is the one who brings my meals. Long after my arrest, he stayed at the roadhouse supervising the work there. Now, he shares the duty, he tells me, with another deputy. They take turns spending a few weeks in the desert. The work has changed him, he says.

He says the miners, too, are replaced from time to time. The bodies at the top of the heap were the easiest to recover. The deeper they go, the more refuse must be mucked out and sorted through. And they recover more bones than bodies. The work weighs on them, as well, I am told. The only stalwart is the miner who runs the steam donkey.

My most frequent visitor is the man who carries the mail to the mining towns. No sooner had we arrived here following my arrest, than he set out again with letters in his saddlebags. He has made several trips since, but says he will soon be out of a job.

It seems the promising vein of ore discovered at one of the old mines more than fulfilled its promise, leading to a large body of gold ripe for recovery. The area is booming again. The mail man tells me the road is busy with traffic—freighters are making regular trips, and miners are using any and every means of conveyance, from shank's mare to horses to mules to handcarts to wagons, to reach the mining town and the promise of work. Storekeepers, barbers, bankers, whores, and others who mine the miners are flocking there. He says the express company is at work getting the road back in shape, and stagecoach—and regular mail—service will soon return to the route.

Most of all, the mail carrier takes some kind of twisted pride in relating news of developments at my roadhouse. He tells me negotiations are underway for the place to resume its former life as a home station for the stage line, with the woman holding the contract. Some Paiutes, kin of some sort to the woman, have taken up residence and are helping with improvements. They are putting up cabins for their own use and to accommodate overnight guests. Installing water lines from the windmill to the roadhouse and the stock pens. (It comes as no surprise to me that they are too lazy to carry water.) Vegetable gardens are under cultivation. The Paiutes brought in, from where he does not know, a herd of well-fed horses, mules, oxen, and beef cattle and are profitably trading with travelers.

It is a mystery to the mail man how the Indians are financing all this. He says they seem to have an unlimited supply of capital, flush with gold and silver coins, and paper currency. As I said, it is a mystery to him—but I have my suspicions. That woman of mine must have been as quiet in her movements as with her mouth and observed from concealment the places where I cached my riches.

Were I to be philosophical about it, I suppose I would be ambivalent about her appropriation of my wealth. But I am not. I pray she falls victim to the biblical prophecy of James: "Your gold and silver is cankered; and the rust of them shall be a witness against you, and shall eat your flesh as it were fire."

In a different sense, that phrase, "a witness against you," is apt to my situation. The bones in the well bear witness against me. All my sins remembered, you might say.

Whether or not those remembered sins haunt my dreams, I do not know. My nights, as always, are often disturbed by dreams that linger in effect, but not memory.

All my sins remembered? Or all my sins forgotten?

Ask me in the morning. Now, to sleep. Perchance to dream.

All is silent. The only sound an insistent hum, or buzz, that seems to emanate from inside his head rather than without. The man stands on a high place, on a wooden platform both solid and unstable beneath his feet. A breeze cools the sweat on his face and riffles his hair. He wants to scratch an itch, a tingle, on his nose but his hands are bound. A crowd of faces below, all eyes locked on him. The faces are familiar, all residing somewhere in the recesses of his memory. Some faces sit atop throats slashed mean, and raw. Others with heads stove in, or cloven. Neat crimson holes pass through flesh and bone to emerge in ragged, gaping voids. Chests shredded; viscera exposed. Faces disappear, and the world closes in, dark and close. The man breathes his own breath. A weight settles on his shoulders, draws snug around his neck. He falls free. A sudden, brilliant flash of whitest light. And then . . .

ABOUT THE AUTHOR

Writer **Rod Miller** is a four-time winner of, and six-time finalist for, the Western Writers of America Spur Award. His writing has also won awards from Western Fictioneers, Westerners International, and the Academy of Western Artists. A lifelong Westerner, Miller writes fiction, history, poetry, and magazine articles about the American West's people and places. Read more online at writerRodMiller.com, awhideRobinson.com, and writerRodMiller.blogspot.com.